Ben the tramp's uncanny knack of running into trouble is unsurpassed in his final hair-raising adventure taking place at No.19, Billiter Road.

Son of novelist Benjamin Farjeon, and brother to children's author Eleanor, playwright Herbert and composer Harry, Joseph Jefferson Farjeon (1883–1955) began work as an actor and freelance journalist before inevitably turning his own hand to writing fiction. Described by the *Sunday Times* as 'a master of the art of blending horrors with humour', Farjeon was a prolific author of mystery novels, with more than 60 books published between 1924 and 1955. His first play, *No. 17*, was produced at the New Theatre in 1925, when the actor Leon M. Lion 'made all London laugh' as Ben the tramp, an unorthodox amateur detective who became the most enduring of all Farjeon's creations. Rewritten as a novel in 1926 and filmed by Alfred Hitchcock six years later, with Mr Lion reprising his role, *No.17*'s success led to seven further books featuring the warm-hearted but danger-prone Ben: 'Ben is not merely a character but a parable—a mixture of Trimalchio and the Old Kent Road, a notable coward, a notable hero, above all a supreme humourist' (Seton Dearden, *Time and Tide*). Although he had become largely forgotten over the 60 years since his death, J. Jefferson Farjeon's reputation made an impressive resurgence in 2014 when his 1937 Crime Club book *Mystery in White* was reprinted by the British Library, returning him to the bestseller lists and resulting in readers wanting to know more about this enigmatic author from the Golden Age of detective fiction.

Also in this series

J. JEFFERSON FARJEON

Number Nineteen

COLLINS
CRIME
CLUB

COLLINS CRIME CLUB

An imprint of HarperCollins*Publishers*
1 London Bridge Street
London SE1 9GF
www.harpercollins.co.uk

This paperback edition 2016

First published in Great Britain for The Crime Club Ltd
by W. Collins Sons & Co. Ltd 1952

A catalogue record for this book is
available from the British Library

ISBN 978-0-00-815606-0

Set in Sabon by Palimpsest Book Production Limited, Falkirk, Stirlingshire

Printed by Clays Ltd, St Ives plc

MIX
Paper from
responsible sources
FSC **FSC˚ C007454**
www.fsc.org

CONTENTS

1

Trouble on a Seat

On a certain grey afternoon he was destined never to forget—he had a packet of them, and he called them his Album of 'Orrers—Ben paused before a park seat, wondered whether to sit down on the unoccupied end or to move on to the next, decided to move on to the next, changed his mind, sat down where he was, and thereby sealed his doom.

It was a pity there was somebody else at the other end of the seat. Ben liked to be alone, because when you're alone no one can bother you, can they? But the man at the other end did not look the bothering kind, and as he was busy with a notebook and it was nice and quiet here, Ben could go on thinking. You could just hear the London traffic in the far distance, but only just, and with all this grass and trees about, well, you might almost be in country, mightn't you?

What was Ben thinking about? If the man at the other end had glanced up from his notebook and made a guess, it was a thousand-to-one chance he would have guessed right, although it so happened this man was good at guessing. When Ben was passing through emotion, and he very frequently was, his thoughts were as plain as the Egyptian Pyramids, but during his contemplative periods there was no knowing what lay behind his glazed, expressionless eyes, which concealed their treasure as the surface of a mine conceals its wealth.

The safest guess was cheese. Ben loved to think of cheese. Though, of course, that came a long way behind eating it. Another possibility was corpses. These he never thought of from choice, but they had a habit of slipping into his mind from that lavish Album of 'Orrers, and—queer, this— there *was* a sort of fascination about them! You couldn't get away from it. You know—once you'd done with them. For instance, take that one he'd found in the cellar in Norgate Road, or the one he'd spoken to on the Embankment, or the one he'd tumbled on in the attic of No. 17—only, of course, that hadn't kep' bein' a corpse, 'ad it? You didn't need a war for Ben to find 'em!

But Ben was not thinking of either corpses or cheese as he sat now on the park seat. He was thinking of numbers, separating the lucky ones from the unlucky ones in the light of his own experience. Seventeen you might call the plum! He wouldn't live in a house numbered seventeen not if you paid him a couple of quid! He always gave the number a miss when he counted. You couldn't call fifteen nice, either. That cellar at Norgate Road had been in Number Fifteen. Thirteen—well, of course, you couldn't ever expect Thirteen to behave itself. He'd known a couple of shockers. And the day he'd found fourteen fag-ends he'd bust his braces, so fourteen was no good, either. Bending dahn fer the last one, that was. Funny how all the 'teens seemed to be against you!

No, the small numbers were best, you couldn't get away from it. Digiots they was called, wasn't they? Take Five. That was nice. It was at a Number Five that a girl had nearly fallen for him. Not quite, but nearly. They never did quite. Golden hair, she'd had, and my, what a wink! Then once he'd bet fivepence on a horse, the only time he'd ever won. And that little kid he'd helped across the road only yesterday. She was five, she told him, when he'd asked her. Yes, Five was nice. Very nice. You couldn't get away from it.

Ben was so busy thinking of the number Five that he did not hear a car stop in a narrow road near where he was sitting. Why should he have paid any attention to it, if he had? It was a quiet road, and the car stopped quietly, as though the driver did not want to disturb the peaceful serenity of the afternoon, or of the two men on the seat, one intent on his notebook, the other gazing at nothing. The driver himself revealed no special characteristic as he began to stroll casually towards the seat. He had dark brown hair and a small moustache. His suit was light grey, and he carried a camera.

He approached quietly. Very quietly indeed. His first view of the two men was of their backs, which meant that neither of them had any view of him at all. He paused when he was within a few yards of them, regarding their backs with, ostensibly, only a vague interest. After a few seconds, during which Ben went on thinking and the man at the other end of the seat went on making his notes, the newcomer turned his head to glance back towards the road. Then he glanced from one side to the other. No one else was in sight. If this gratified the newcomer his expression did not register the fact. His expression, indeed, was rather bored.

Continuing his stroll, he veered a little in his route and came round Ben's end of the seat. Ben saw him now out of the corner of his eye, but was still too absorbed in his recollection of the little girl of five to be diverted by a glimpse of a casual stroller. It was not until the newcomer had walked a little farther on and, turning, raised the camera he was carrying that he was in full view. Ben lifted his head just as the camera clicked, and a distant clock chimed four.

'Wozzat for?' he blinked. 'Television?'

'No. Just for my private collection,' answered the photographer, with a faint smile.

'Oh! Well, if my phiz is goin' in, yer better keep it privit!' grunted Ben.

'I hope you didn't mind? I just couldn't resist. I specialise in studies in contrast.'

His turn to take the snapshot had brought him facing the direction from which he had come, and now he began walking back towards the road. Unless he had left his car especially to get this picture, which on the face of it seemed hardly likely, his short stroll appeared somewhat pointless. The man with the notebook had stopped writing at the sound of voices, without looking up. Now he suddenly closed the book and slipped it in his pocket. He was bringing out his cigarette-case as the photographer was returning by the seat, passing it this time at his end.

What happened immediately afterwards was never completely clear in Ben's mind. One obvious reason was the particular nature of the happenings, but another lay in the fact that the photographer had disturbed his thoughts and he was trying to get back into them. What had he been thinking about? Oh, yus, that little gal and Nummer

Five. Nice little kid, and no mistake. He liked 'em that age. They knew just enough to get on with and they hadn't learned yet to be cheeky. Not that this little girl looked like ever getting cheeky. No, she wasn't that kind. He'd watched her standing there, waiting to get across—fancy lettin' 'er aht alone, 'er mother didn't ought!—and when he'd gone up to her she had put her hand in his, trusting him like he might be anybody. He'd like to have bought her some sweets, but he hadn't no coupons, and even if he had, how far would tuppence go? Besides, nice little girls weren't supposed to take things from strangers, or even to talk to 'em, and there was that there time when he'd said it was a nice day to a small child, brown hair she had, and her mother had pulled her away sharp . . .

Even more sharply, Ben pulled his mind back from the past to the present. Oi! Wot was 'appenin'? That photographer bloke hadn't gone. He'd stopped again—come round the back of the seat—and was standing behind the man with the notebook, with his hand raised . . . Oi! Look aht!

Ben tried to shriek the words, but no words came. They stuck in his throat, which had become constricted with horror, and before he could make a second effort the man slumped forward with a knife in his back. Out of a corner of the glazed eye that was glued on that murderous knife Ben glimpsed the notebook slipping down to the ground.

'Corse, this ain't 'appenin'!' decided Ben, making a miserable and familiar effort to wipe out reality. 'Yer don't go murderin' folk not in public daylight, and afore witnessesses! Well, do yer?'

The answer came in the form of the murderer's face. It suddenly loomed larger than life before Ben's own. It looked so large it seemed to fill the universe.

'Wot I gotter do,' thought Ben, 'is ter 'it it.'

With a face that size, it was impossible to miss. But just as Ben's throat had gone off duty when it was needed, so now did Ben's fist. He tried to raise it, and found it powerless.

'I gorn numb,' he concluded.

He had. Not only his fist, but every part of him. The sardonic face was draining all the strength out of him, and seemed now to be curling round him, as though he were imprisoned inside it. If only he could get free for a moment, lummy, he'd show it! Hit and run—hit and run—hit and run! But there was no escape from this facial cage, and even the moustache had grown to a mile in length and seemed to be binding him . . . And now wasn't there a second face? Smaller—vaguer—but somewhere about. And what was that prick in his arm? Had that happened this moment, or very long ago? Long ago—yes, of course—very long ago. Because after that—don't you remember—there was that little golden-haired girl. You saw her standing there and wanting to get across the road, and you went up to her and said, 'I'll tike yer across, missie,' and she put her hand in yours, trusting you jest like you might be anybody . . .

2

More Trouble on a Bed

When Ben opened his eyes he decided that he was still asleep. You often wake from one dream into another, and it was of course quite impossible that he should be lying like this on a bed. Wasn't he on a park seat, and even if he had rolled off the seat because of something that had happened—and he felt sure something had happened, though his mind was too muzzy to recall just what it was—he would have rolled off on to the grass, well, wouldn't he? He wouldn't have bounced into a bedroom, because even though Ben was good at bouncing he couldn't bounce quite as far as that.

And there was another thing that proved this must be a dream. He could just see the tip of one of his boots, and it wasn't his boot. His boots were old and shabby; in fact one of them, owing to sundry gaps, could hardly be called a boot at all. You just put your foot in and it came out at the other end. But this boot he could see the tip of—yes, it was the left boot, the one with the gap—had no gap at all. Nor did it look old and worn. It was miraculously

7

complete, and there was even a bit of polish on it. So, well, there you were. It was just another dream.

He hoped it would prove a nice one. He had an idea that the preceding dream had not been so good. If he lay very still, so as not to disturb it, a door might open somewhere and the Prime Minister might come in. And he might say, 'Don't move, Ben. I know you're feeling bad—' he was '—but you did a noble act dashing in front of that car and saving that little girl from being run over. You might of got killed. Well, England doesn't forget brave acts like that, so we're going to reward you with Ten Thousand Pounds—' Yes, that would be a very nice dream.

He closed his eyes, and waited for it. But the Prime Minister did not oblige. A door did open somewhere, however, and suddenly feeling convinced that it did not herald the arrival of anyone so beneficent as a grateful Premier, Ben opened his eyes again quickly, jest to be ready like. Again he saw that impossible, polished toe. He still believed he was dreaming, but he was sure by now that the dream was not going to be a nice one.

The person who had come in had entered by a door behind the bed. He seemed in no hurry—assuming it was a 'he'—for after closing the door there was no further sound for a full minute. Then the approaching footsteps were resumed, reached the bed, and continued round the foot of it. Then they ceased again, and Ben found himself regarding no longer the surprisingly polished boot but the face above it, and as he gazed, remembrance came flooding back. It was the face of the man with the dark brown hair and the small moustache. The face that had enveloped him before his black-out.

'This,' decided Ben, 'is goin' ter be narsty!'

For a few moments the two men regarded each other silently. It was Ben who broke the silence.

'Go on! Let's 'ave it!' he muttered.

'Ah, you have recovered your voice,' replied the other. 'Have what?'

'Wot it's orl abart!'

'But you, of all people, should know what it is all about?'

Ben gulped, then tried to steady himself. Things was wobblin' somethink 'orrerble!

'I knows a bit,' he said, guardedly.

'And what bit do you refer to?' came the enquiry.

'Do yer need me ter tell yer?'

'I am asking you to tell me.'

Ben gulped again.

'Orl right, guv'ner, 'ere goes. I knows that summon's bin murdered!'

'Murdered?'

'Does it surprise yer?'

'It's a nasty word, but—no, I cannot say, truthfully, that it surprises me.'

'It wouldn't. See, yer was there, wasn't yer?'

'And so, I gather, were you?'

'I was.'

'Then of course you will know who did it?'

'I knows.'

'Then perhaps you would tell me?'

'Yer want me ter say?'

'I should be interested. It was a shocking thing, was it not? Who *did* do it?'

Ben swallowed, to clear his throat for the next. Of course the man knew Ben knew who had done it, but it is never

9

pleasant to inform a murderer of his crime, especially when there is nobody else about.

'You did it,' said Ben.

'Come, come!' smiled the man.

'That ain't no good,' retorted Ben. 'I seen yer!'

'I'm afraid that is no good, either,' answered the man, 'for is it not just what anybody in your position would say?'

'Eh? In my persishun?' repeated Ben, blinking. 'I don't git yer?'

The man continued to smile. It was one of the least pleasant smiles Ben had ever seen.

'Please do not disappoint me, my good man. I credited you with some intelligence. Are you speaking the truth? Don't you really and truly get me?'

And then, all at once, Ben did, and sweat appeared upon his brow.

'Yer—yer ain't meanin'—?' he began, but he was interrupted before he got any farther.

'Let us go slowly,' said the man. 'Sometimes it is not quite wise to say exactly what one means. We have plenty of time, and as this is going to be a long conversation, I think I will take a chair.'

He turned away and walked towards a chair in the corner of the room. How about a dash while his back was turned? Ben had not heard a key turn, so evidently the door was not locked. Yes, that was it! A couple of leaps and then 'ell for leather! He wouldn't get another chance.

But unfortunately Ben was not in a condition for leaping. He could only leap in spirit; his body refused to oblige. Lummy, he didn't half feel weak!

'There is a mirror on this wall,' remarked the man, as

he reached the chair, 'and I have something in my pocket which would get to the door before you possibly could. As a matter of fact, it would pass through you on its way. Let me repeat my advice. Take things slowly. You may find—if you are sensible—that your position has its saving graces.'

'Savin' 'oo?' muttered Ben.

As the man returned with the chair his teeth became prominent below his little moustache. He smiled with his teeth.

'Do you know, I rather like you,' he said. 'What is your name?'

'Winston Churchill,' replied Ben. You might as well die game. 'Wot's your'n?'

'I won't respond with Clement Attlee. If you want something to call me—'

'I could call yer plenty withaht no 'elp!'

'I have no doubt you could, but I suggest Mr Smith. What am I to call you? I confess I find Winston Churchill rather a mouthful.'

'Orl right. Yer can call me Jones.'

'That being your real name?'

'As much as I reckon Smith is your'n!'

'Very well. Then that is settled—for the moment. I am Smith and you are Jones, and we are discussing the demise—or death, if you prefer simple terms—of a third party who so far has to be nameless.' He sat down by the bed. 'Oh, but perhaps you can tell me his name?'

'Corse I carn't!' retorted Ben. ''Ow'd I know it?'

'Well, it occurred to me that you might, since you were so obviously interested in him?'

''Ow was I interested in 'im?'

11

'That is what I hope to learn, for only lunatics—and I haven't yet decided that you are a lunatic, though it is a theory—only lunatics attack perfect strangers—'

'Nah, then, I don't want no more o' that!' interrupted Ben, with anxious indignation. 'I never seed the bloke afore in me life, and you ain't goin' ter put that on me!'

Mr Smith shook his head reprovingly.

'I fear you are getting me all wrong,' he said. 'I am not putting anything on you—or, more correctly speaking, what I put on you need not matter. Your headache, Mr Jones, is what the police may put on you, and that actually is what you and I have got to discuss.'

'The pleece carn't put nothink on me!'

'I wish I could agree.'

'Well, as I didn't do it—'

'Somebody did it!'

'Yus, but we ain't torkin' abart anyone else jest nah, we're torkin' abart me, and as I didn't do it *I* ain't got ter worry abart the pleece!'

Mr Smith gave a little sigh, turned his head for a moment towards the door, and then turned it back again.

'You really are being very difficult, Mr Jones,' he complained. 'Here I am, trying to help you—'

'Oh, 'elp me, is it?'

'Can't you see?'

'I couldn't see that withaht a telerscope!'

'You say the most delightful things. My desire to help you increases every moment, and the best way to prove it is to explain to you precisely what your position is, and what the police could put on you if you had the misfortune to meet them. I am afraid we can no longer mince matters, Mr Jones, and we shall *have* to say exactly what we mean, after all. And, come to think of it, you didn't mince matters when you attempted to put the murder on *me*! Not many would forgive you for that, yet here am I, still sticking to you! Now, then, let us begin. You deny, I understand, that you stabbed the man on the other end of your seat?'

"Ow many more times?' growled Ben.

'One of your troubles, of course, is that you cannot prove an alibi. You know what an alibi is?'

'Yus. It's when yer can prove yer wasn't where they say yer was.'

'Correct. If ever you write a dictionary I shall buy a copy. And you cannot prove that you were not on that seat.'

'Come ter that, 'oo could prove I was?'

'Well—I could!'

'That's not sayin' they'd believe yer.'

'No, but then I could prove you were, if my word wasn't good enough.'

"Ow could yer?'

'You have a very short memory. Don't you remember that, a few moments before the tragedy, I took a photograph?'

'Lummy, so yer did!'

'The police might give a lot for a copy of that photograph. Don't you agree?'

Ben offered no opinion.

'And then,' went on Mr Smith, 'there is something else you ought to know. That horrible knife sticking in the poor man's back—I had to leave it there, for I had not the nerve to take it out—horrible, horrible!—the police will naturally examine the handle, and they will find your fingerprints upon it.'

13

'Wot's that?' gasped Ben.

'You really ought to have wiped them off,' said Mr Smith, sadly. 'You can be quite sure that, if *I* had done the deed, I would have wiped mine off! You might like to make a note of that. Oh, no! Oh, no! I would never have left mine on!'

'But mine carn't be on!' cried Ben, desperately.

'Not so loud, not so loud!' admonished Mr Smith. 'I assure you, Mr Jones, your fingerprints are on that knife. You may deny it till you are blue in the face. It will make no difference. The fingerprints are there.'

'Owjer know?'

'A needless question, surely? I was present at the tragedy. I saw the deed, and I know you did not wipe the knife-handle after using it.'

Ben shut his eyes hard to think. It was easier in the dark, without Mr Smith's face before him. First the photograph—and now the fingerprints. Clearly Mr Smith had not left his own prints on the knife; he had told Ben to make a note of this, and he was far too wily a customer to commit such a cardinal blunder. But he had not merely wiped his fingerprints off, he had apparently stamped Ben's on! While he was unconscious! He'd worked the whole thing out from the word go . . .

'Are you asleep?' came Mr Smith's voice.

If only he had been! Apprehensively and slowly, Ben opened his eyes.

'So you see,' went on Mr Smith smoothly, as though there had been no interruption, 'you are in a bit of a hole, are you not?'

'S'pose I am?' answered Ben.

'There is no suppose about it. You are. And you will be

14

in a worse hole if, in addition to the fingerprints, I am unable to prevent that photograph from appearing in all the newspapers—a photograph of a murdered man on one end of a seat with another man wanted for enquiries at the other. You say you never saw the murdered man before today?'

'Never in me life,' replied Ben.

He knew this was a frame-up, but would it be wise to let Mr Smith know he knew? Perhaps he'd better lie doggo for a bit—stop makin' a fuss like—and act as though he thought Mr Smith were really trying to help him, until he found out where it was all leading?

'Then why did you kill him?'

Still wavering as to his best policy, and with his mind beginning to rocket again, Ben could not answer that one and remained silent. He was stunned by the cool audacity of Mr Smith, who now bent forward and continued, almost confidentially.

'Do you know, I've got a theory about this murder of yours, and you need not tell me whether I am right or wrong. As a matter of fact, it was because of my idea that I brought you along here instead of handing you over to the police, as of course I ought to have done. Oh, don't make any mistake, I am taking a big risk myself in acting like this—but let that go. I like to help people in trouble—if they're worth it, of course—and the reason I'm helping you is because I feel sure yours wasn't a premeditated murder.'

'Pre 'oo?' blinked Ben.

'You didn't set out to murder this poor fellow,' explained Mr Smith, 'as—for instance—I might have done if I had been the culprit. You were ill, perhaps. Or hungry. I don't

15

know—don't ask me! But all at once everything got on top of you, eh? You had a brain-storm. As a matter of fact, Mr Jones, that's just what it *looked* like to me! A brain-storm. And you jumped upon your poor victim with that knife, perhaps hardly knowing you did it—why, you even thought *I* did it, which proves the brain-storm, doesn't it—and then—I suppose you know this?—you had a complete black-out! Well, as my car was handy, for I'd only left it a minute or two before to have a tiny stroll, I acted upon a sudden impulse and bundled you off while the going was good. Of course, there'll be a big hue and cry for you later, if it hasn't already started. You'd never have left those fingerprints on the knife if you'd been normal. They'll damn you, I'm afraid. But you're safe here, for the time being, so now what we've got to decide is what I'm going to do with you.' He displayed his teeth in another of his unpleasant smiles. 'Have you any idea?'

Guardedly Ben responded,

''Ave you?'

'As a matter of fact I have, but first let me ask you a question or two. A lot will depend on your answers. Let us hope for your sake they will be satisfactory.'

'S'pose they ain't?'

'That will be just too bad. Now, then. Is anybody likely to trail you here? Apart, of course, from the police?'

''Owjer mean?'

'I speak the King's English. Have you any people who will wonder why you haven't gone home tonight?'

'Oh, I see.'

'Well, have you?'

'No one never worries abart me, and if they did, 'ow'd they find me? I dunno where I am meself!'

16

'Where do you live?'

'Where I 'appen to be.'

'Try again. What's your address?'

'Nothink doin', guv'nor! I knows that one!'

'What one?'

'I seen it done. Yer gits a bloke away wot's wanted, and then yer gits a messidge to 'is wife or 'is muvver that yer'll give 'im up unless they sends yer a pony.'

'You know, you're smarter than you look,' said Mr Smith, admiringly. 'If I weren't straight I'd begin to watch my step. Will it ease you if I promise not to communicate with your wife or mother?'

'Yer couldn't, 'cos I ain't got 'em,' answered Ben.

'I am full of patience. Who have you got?'

'I told yer. Nobody.'

'Where did you sleep last night?'

'In a bus.'

'But when you got out of the bus?'

'I'd 'ad it by then, it was mornin'.'

'Tell me, Mr Jones. Does all this mean you haven't got any address?'

'That's right. Two and two's four. And if that ain't a satisfact'ry answer, I've 'ad it.'

'It is an exceedingly satisfactory answer,' Mr Smith assured him. 'If you have no home and no family you should be free to accept the position I'm thinking of offering you.'

'Oh! A persishun?'

'That is what I said.'

'A standin' up one? Not lyin' in a bed?'

'Or hanging from a rope.'

'Oi! That's enuff o' that!'

'It is an alternative we want to bear in mind.'

'Well, wot's the persishun?'

'Quite a simple one, and just the thing, I should say for you. We've—er—lost our caretaker, and we need a new one.'

3

Mr Smith v. Mr Jones

The announcement of this surprising offer was followed by a silence during which the alleged Mr Smith and the alleged Mr Jones would have given much to have been inside the other's mind. What lay in the background of Mr Smith's mind was obscure, but what lay in the foreground was actually quite simple. He was studying his victim to learn his reaction, and was ready to deal with him by other methods if the reaction did not appear satisfactory.

What lay in Ben's mind ran something like this:

'Wozzat? Caretaiker did 'e say? Wozzat mean? Wot'd 'e want with me as 'is caretaiker, a bloke wot 'e sez 'e thinks 'as done a murder, if it wasn't fishy? Fishy? Corse it's fishy! Look at me bein' 'ere like I am, and knowin' 'e done it 'iself, and 'im knowin' I know! Fishy the pair of us, if yer looks at it like that! Yus, and even if I 'ad done it, not premedicated wot 'e sed, I'd be barmy, and wot do yer want with a barmy caretaiker? It don't mike sense! Oi, keep yer fice steady, Ben! Don't let on wot yer thinkin'

from yer phiz, 'cos 'e's watchin' ter find aht, sime as yer
watchin' 'im. 'Ow I 'ates 'is mustarch! I carn't think o'
nothin' nicer'n ter pull it orf! P'r'aps it'd come orf easy?
Yus, I bet it would, it ain't 'is mustarch no more'n Smith's
'is nime. Sime as that bloke with the 'orrerble beard in
that 'ouse in Brixton and when I got 'old of it it come orf
bing in me 'and and I goes back'ards dahn the stairs with
nothin' but the beard on top o' me! And then there was
that chap with the red eyebrows—oi! Wotcher doin'? Keep
yer mind on it! Yer ain't in Brixton now, yer 'ere, wherever
that is, and wot yer tryin' ter do is ter work aht why yer
wanted as caretaiker, but 'ow can yer with yer 'ead goin'
rahnd like a spinging-wheel and feelin' as if yer got no
knees, and wunnerin' why yer boot's gorn bright and
polished, lummy, I've 'ad a dose o' somethink, yer carn't
git away from it! . . .'

Difficult as Mr Smith's mind may have been to read,
Mr Jones's was even more complicated.

When the silence was threatening to become permanent,
Mr Smith broke it monosyllabically.

'Well?'

Ben came to with a jerk.

'Say it agine,' answered Ben.

'It was so long ago I'm not surprised if you've forgotten.
I said we needed a new caretaker.'

'There was somethink helse.'

'Was there?'

'I ain't fergot that.'

'Then you might remind me?'

'Yer sed yer'd lorst the old 'un.'

'So I did.'

'Well, 'ow did yer lose 'im?'

Mr Smith did not respond at once. The question seemed both to interest and surprise him. A very faint smile entered his expression when he replied.

'You're a careful one, aren't you, Mr Jones?'

'If yer wanter learn somethink,' retorted Ben, 'I ain't sich a fool as I look!'

He hoped his tone was convincing. Mr Smith's smile grew a little more distinct.

'That, if you will forgive me,' he returned, 'would be difficult. Although perhaps you have no precise idea at this moment how you do look—but we will return to that later.'

'That's okay by me if we can return nah to that hother caretaiker. Wot 'appened ter 'im?'

'Ah!'

'That don't tell me nothink.'

'It was not intended to. I only intend to tell you—that is, until I have learned to know you a little better—what is strictly necessary. But I see no reason why I should not tell you that our last caretaker was not a very good one.'

'Meanin' that 'e didn't keep the plice clean, or go ter the door when the bell rang?'

'What else should I mean?'

'That's wot I'm arskin'.'

'Then let us put it this way. He proved disappointing— after, I admit, a very good start—in not completely fulfilling his job.'

'And s'pose I don't fulfil my job?'

'That would be a pity for both of us. You see, Mr Jones, however well you started—and you are not really making such a bad beginning—you would have to keep it up. You would have to prove yourself trustworthy. In that way, you might eventually be given more responsibility, and end up by doing quite well for yourself. Do you get that?'

'P'r'aps I do, and p'r'aps I don't,' answered Ben, cautiously, 'but wot I don't git is wot's goin' ter 'appen ter me if I don't turn aht more satisfact'ry than t'other chap? See, that was why I arsked yer wot 'appened ter '*im*?'

Mr Smith shook his head.

'I would not press that,' he said.

''Oo's pressin' wot?' replied Ben. 'Orl right, jest tell me this. If I ain't no good in this job, will I be free ter go and git another?'

'You are more tenacious, Mr Jones, than a tiger with a hunk of juicy meat, but let me warn you that I am growing tired of these questions. You would be no more free to go and get another job than you are free at this moment to go and get any job. You forget that you have just done one job on a park seat from the consequences of which I am—so far—saving you. I shall only continue in this Christian mood so long as you yourself continue to give satisfaction in the new job I am now offering you.'

'I see. And so that's really why yer brort me along? It wasn't jest 'cos yer was sorry fer me like? Okay, that's orl right by me, on'y if I'm goin' ter work fer yer I likes ter start straight—no matter 'ow crooked we git laiter on,' he added, with a wink which he hoped was impressive. He must not appear too virtuous, for that clearly would be of no use to him. 'So let's 'ear wot I gotter do?'

'Then you accept the job?'

'Well, I dunno as I'm up ter it, not afore yer tells me?'

'True,' nodded Mr Smith. 'But I feel sure you will be up to it, for—to start with—you will find it quite simple. This house is in the market to be sold. Sold as it stands, with everything in it. Some of the rooms are furnished, some are not. You will keep those that are furnished reasonably tidy. You will not be dismissed, however, if you leave a few cobwebs. Personally I rather like cobwebs. Do you? Nor need you exert yourself chasing spiders. There are a number of spiders here, some quite large ones. I rather like spiders, too. Beetles, for some occult reason, I am less fond of. There is one room here practically devoted to them. A small room at the back, with three loose boards. But in spite of the condition of the house, and the livestock, a big price is being asked for it, because it is really a valuable property—' he paused, and an odd expression came into his face '—yes, a very valuable property, and so we are waiting until somebody comes along who realises its worth. But the price, of course, has nothing to do with you.'

'No, I ain't buyin' it,' said Ben.

'That I hardly expected, and I merely mentioned it in case any people who are sent here by the agent make any comments about the price which you otherwise would not understand. The agent is Wavell and Son. The original Wavell died recently, and it is the son who carries on. You may meet him some day, but that is not very likely. He rarely comes here himself, but just sends his clients on with a list, which includes this house among others on his books. Wavell and Son. Make a note of it. The address does not matter to you.'

Mr Smith paused, as though considering what else to tell his new caretaker. Ben took advantage of the pause to put a question.

'No, the address of the agent don't matter ter me,' he

said, 'but it wouldn't 'urt ter know the address of the 'ouse I'm lookin' arter.'

'That certainly would not hurt,' Mr Smith agreed. 'The house is in Billiter Road, and the number is Nineteen.'

'Oh! Nummer Nineteen?'

'Anything wrong with it?'

There was a lot wrong with it. Earlier that day Ben had been cogitating over numbers, sorting out the lucky ones from the unlucky ones, and as we know he had decided that all the teen-numbers boded no good!

'If there is, I carn't alter it,' he replied. 'Okay. This is Nummer 19, Billiter Road, and it's fer sale at a top price, spiders and orl, and the agent is Wavell and Son. I got orl that. Wot's next?'

'You will answer the bell and then leave whoever comes to go over the house, staying here in this room till they have gone—unless otherwise instructed. The bell is all you will answer. You are not here to answer questions. Or, for that matter, to ask them.'

'Why should I arsk 'em?'

'That was one. I am telling you you shouldn't. In fact, Mr Jones, you must restrain your bump of curiosity in every possible way, on every possible subject. You will remain in the house, and you will not leave it until you receive permission.'

Ben considered this last instruction. It had its virtues. He did not want to go out—for a while, at any rate. There might be a policeman at the corner, and although he could go up to him and say, if the policeman did not speak to him first, 'I'm caretaker fer the bloke wot murdered the man on the park seat,' it was his, Ben's fingerprints that were on the knife, and the truth about them would appear a somewhat tall story. Though, admittedly, it might be to prevent the opportunity for such a statement that Mr Smith wanted his caretaker confined to the house.

But there were objections to staying perpetually indoors. One was the obvious one of shopping. How was Ben going to buy his food? Yes, and how about the money to buy it with? The question of salary had not yet been raised.

He dealt with these two important points in order.

''Ere's a cupple o' questions fer yer, if I should arsk 'em or not,' he said. 'Fust, I gotter eat? Ain't I ter go ter no shops?'

'There is some tinned stuff in the larder,' replied Mr Smith, 'and as I shall call periodically, you can always tell me if there is anything you need.'

'I see. You does me shoppin' for me, like?'

'Won't that be kind of me?'

'So long as yer don't fergit me supper beer. Wot's periodic? Wot time do I expeck yer?'

'When you see me.'

'Oh! Yer couldn't mike it a reg'ler time?'

'Why?'

'Well, I jest thort it'd be more convenient like.'

'More convenient for you to slip out and get that supper beer? No, Mr Jones, we will not make it a regular time.'

Ben gave that one up, and tried the next.

''Ow much are yer payin' me?' he asked. 'Ten pahnd a week?'

'I am not paying you anything,' answered Mr Smith. 'Not at the start, anyway. Later on, if you are good, I may raise your wages.'

'Yer carn't raise wot I ain't got!'

'Aren't you a devil for accuracy?'

'I dunno wot that means, but I never worked fer nothink afore. Fer standin' in front of a 'orse yer gits tuppence!'

'You will not be working for nothing. You will receive both food and shelter, and since you cannot go out, what would you spend your pocket money on?'

Then Ben gave that one up, too. But all at once he thought of another question, and it hit him bang in the middle of his stomach.

'Guv'ner,' he said. 'Yer ain't sent that photo ter the pleece, 'ave yer?'

'As a matter of fact, I shall probably do so,' replied Mr Smith. 'Yes, thinking matters over, I am inclined to believe it will be the wisest plan.'

Indignation mingled with apprehension in Ben's breast as he heard this callous statement.

'Wot! Send it orf, arter yer sed—?'

'I made no promise.'

'P'r'aps yer didn't, but it'll put a spanner in the works! Wot's the good of engaigin' me fer yer caretaiker if yer 'ave me 'auled orf ter the pleece stashun?'

Mr Smith laughed. Ben's indignation grew. For the first time he raised himself and sat up, glaring at Mr Smith with challenging eyes.

'Yer wants it both ways, doncher?' he exclaimed. 'Well, yer carn't 'ave it, 'cos it won't work, see? I expeck that's why I ain't ter go aht of the 'ouse, in caise I'm reckernised from the photo, as I would be, not 'avin' a ordinary fice like your'n that might be anyone's—'

'But you aren't going out of the house—'

'Yus, I knows that! But wot abart them 'ouse-'unters wot I've gotter show over? Ave yer fergot *them*? They'll reckernise me—'

26

'Oh, no, they won't,' Mr Smith interrupted again. And again he laughed. 'Have a look at yourself.'

He went to the wall and brought back the mirror, thrusting it before Ben's face. Ben gazed at himself in stupefaction. This wasn't him! It was another feller! And—lummy!—he had on a clean dark suit, and brightly polished boots!

4

Transformation Scene

'Well, how do you like yourself?' enquired Mr Smith. Ben continued to stare at the strange face in the mirror, and the strange face in the mirror continued to stare back. He was not yet ready to reply. He was afraid that when he did so he might find his voice had changed, too!

'Personally I think that smooth black hair suits you,' went on Mr Smith, 'and your side-whiskers give you an air of distinction that was quite lacking when I first met you. I am sure that when your photograph appears tomorrow over the caption, "Wanted," no one will recognise you as the original of that picture. The only thing I have been unable to change,' he added, with a little sigh, 'is your fingerprints. Come, say something! Aren't you grateful?'

'I dunno,' muttered Ben, finding his voice at last, and relieved at its familiar sound.

'Well, you ought to be,' answered Mr Smith reprovingly. 'I took a lot of trouble over you, and there is very little chance now that you will be recognised by any who call here—although, of course, if you are recognised by any unfortunate chance, the fact that you have changed your appearance will be further evidence against you.'

'But it was you wot done it,' Ben pointed out.

'I should make no claim—the credit would all be yours! As a matter of fact, a friend did help me. Changing your clothes was, in the circumstances, a two-man job. During your black-out you gave us no help at all.'

'Oh! Yer did it while I was subconscious?'

'I accept your term for it.'

'And there's another one of yer?'

'You refer to my friend?'

''Oo is 'e?'

'If I told you his name you would be no wiser.'

'Oh! Well, where is 'e now?'

'Don't worry about him.'

'No, I ain't got nothink ter worry abart, 'ave I? Was 'e in the park with yer?'

'He was in the car. We were out for a little drive together. Tell me. How are you feeling?'

'Jest as if I'd come back from a 'ollerday at Brighton.'

'That's fine. Then I needn't worry about your physical condition before I go?'

'Oh—yer goin'?' said Ben.

'I do not live here,' answered Mr Smith.

'That's right. If yer did, yer could be yer own caretaiker.'

'You've put it in a nutshell.'

Ben blinked as a new realisation suddenly dawned on him.

'Yer mean—when yer go I'll be 'ere orl by meself?'

'Well, I wouldn't say that exactly.'

'Oh! Oo's me company then?'

'Those spiders and black beetles.'

'Shurrup!'

'And I forgot to mention a giant rat. The last caretaker called him Goliath, so you can act the part of David if you meet him. I'm sorry I can't supply you with a sling and stone, but you may find a brick or two around the place.'

'Do you know wot yer torkin' abart?'

'You evidently don't. Not biblical minded, eh? I'd better bring you a copy of the Bible—you'll have plenty of time to read. Now, then, before I go, have you any questions to ask?'

'I thort I wasn't ter arsk none!' retorted Ben.

'You can ask me, but nobody else. You see, Mr Jones, I shall only answer those I choose. So if you've got any bullets, shoot!'

Ben just saved himself from remarking, 'I wish I 'ad!' After all, whether he were believed or not by his enigmatic employer the time had come when he must appear to be willing. No other policy would work.

''Ere's one,' he said. 'Wot time do we open?'

'I'm not engaging you to run a shop.'

'Yus, but them 'ouse-'unters ain't goin' ter turn up fer breakfust?'

'Hardly likely.'

'Or arter I gorn ter bed?'

'That might depend on what time you go to bed.'

'Well, see, that's wot I wanter know. Even a caretaiker 'as ter 'ave a bit o' time orf.'

'I believe the agent opens at nine and closes at about five or six—'

'Ah, nah we're gittin' it!'

'But as, unless he accompanies his clients, he merely gives them a list of addresses, they may call at any time.'

'Oh! And s'pose they mike the time midnight?'

'Your duty will be to admit them whenever they call.'

'I see. In me perjarmers!'

'Did you bring any pyjamas? Don't make trouble before you get it. If it comes it will come without your asking. Next, or is that the lot?'

'Well, p'r'aps it wouldn't be a bad idea,' suggested Ben, 'if yer was ter show me over the 'ouse? Arter orl, I'd look silly if I was ter 'ave ter show people over it afore I'd bin over it meself?'

'You are not expected to act as an official guide. You will not have to tell people, "This is where you eat. This is where you sleep. This is where the coal goes. This room's haunted." The rooms will speak for themselves. You will merely open the front door, and then let your visitors roam where they like. Do not follow them about. I've told you that. You return here to your room. If anything—unusual happens, make no trouble about it, and accept it without question. You can always give me a report when I come along myself. Have you got that quite clear?'

'No.'

'What don't you understand?'

'Wot's goin' ter 'appen that ain't ushueral?'

'How can I tell you before it happens? I am just warning you to be prepared for it if it does happen, and to take it all calmly and coolly. Of course you are free to go over the house after I have gone, and this brings me to my own last point. You will find one door locked. Don't worry about that. All the rest are open to you.'

31

'Oh! So one door's locked, is it?' blinked Ben.

Mr Smith made no response.

'And I ain't ter worry abart it?'

Mr Smith did not seem to be listening. At least, not to Ben.

'Orl right, on'y s'pose—?'

'Stay here—I'll be back in a minute,' said Mr Smith, and quietly left the room.

It was a disturbing as well as a sudden departure. What had he gone off like that for? And suppose he wasn't back in a minute? How long was Ben expected to stay like he was. Not that he had any inclination to move, but as the seconds went by, and Ben counted more than sixty, he found it exceedingly unnerving waiting helplessly in bed. Eighty-four, eighty-five, eighty-six . . . 'ow many more? Eighty-nine, a 'undred, no, ninety, ninety-one, ninety-two. And then, s'pose, when 'e comes back, it ain't 'im? Ben had known that happen before. An Indian goes out, and a Chinaman comes in! Yer never know, do yer? Ninety-eight, ninety-nine . . . lummy, wot was that? Sahnded like a cry! But he wasn't sure. Ben often heard things that weren't. Yus, but this thumpin' ain't imaginashinon! *Thud-thud, thud-thud, thud-thud*. Oi, it's gittin' louder, and faster! Why 'ad 'is farver and muvver ever met? 'Underd-and-five, 'underd-and-six, 'underd-and-seven . . . *thud-thud, thud-thud, thud-thud* . . .

'Gawd! It's me bloody 'eart!'

He lay back weakly and closed his eyes. Or—was it? He opened his eyes. Mr Smith was standing at the foot of his bed again.

'You were saying?' enquired Mr Smith.

'I've fergot,' gulped Ben.

'I think I know. You were going to ask what you should do if any house-hunters want to go into the room with the locked door? Quite simple. You will tell them—if they ask you, otherwise why worry?—that the owner uses it for storage and has taken away the key. Well, that's all. I'll be seeing you tomorrow. Happy sleep.'

And then Mr Smith went away again, and Ben heard the sound of the front door closing.

5

Behind the Locked Door

Well, here he was! And the question he had to solve, while he lay on the bed and contemplated his unenviable position, was whether to stay or whether to cut and run?

He weighed the two alternatives in his own peculiar fashion. S'pose he cut and run? Where'd he run to? And if he couldn't think of anywhere—and he couldn't—when he stopped he'd find himself somewhere, and what would he do with his face? Not to mention his suit? If he got rid of his face, which he might do in a public lavatory, though even so it would be tricky—if he got rid of his face and regained his own, his own would not fit his posh suit, and he could not get rid of his suit without being subsequently arrested for wandering about in an immodest condition. He was quite sure that his own clothing, such as it was, had been confiscated by the much too thorough Mr Smith.

Then there were other arguments against cutting and running. One, he was a suspect, and would soon be on the 'wanted' list for murder. Two, would he get farther than the street? 'I bet that bloke's watchin' the front door!'

he reflected. 'Or if 'e ain't, that friend of 'is is! Don't fergit, there's more'n one of 'em in this set-up, even if yer ain't seed more'n the one so fur!' And, three—and this alone could have been the deciding factor—he really didn't feel up to cutting and running. His knees felt that weak, and he was all wobblin' inside like.

The arguments against staying were, of course, equally numerous. It was goin' to be no picnic, getting entangled in Mr Smith's affairs. Why, lummy, he'd be workin' for a murderer! And how was that going to look, when it came out? 'Corse, I wasn't reely workin' fer 'im, sir, if yer git me. See, I was cornered proper, so I thort if I 'ung on fer a bit I might turn the taibles like, and find aht wot 'e was up ter. Well, that wasn't goin' against the pleece, was it? No, it was tryin' ter 'elp 'em!' As Ben imagined himself explaining himself thus to a police inspector, he was struck with the force of his own argument. It was all too completely true. He *was* cornered . . . and he *did* want to turn the tables on Mr Smith . . . but, continuing with the arguments against staying, there were those beetles and spiders, how he hated them both, and that rat, and there was that locked door. And *had* that been a cry he had heard?

It was not beyond reason to expect, if he stayed, an exceedingly creepy night.

Then, quite suddenly, came two visions that settled the matter for him. The first was of a larder containing tinned food. He needed food, and the need would increase, and was there any food for him outside? He slipped his hands into his trouser pockets—strangely clean and holeless—to find them, as expected, empty. Mr Smith was hardly likely to have left him with any money!

But the second vision, though it did not arise out of any personal need, he found even more compelling. It was of the man at the other end of the park seat. At one moment, quietly making notes in a notebook. At the next, limp, with a knife in his back. Ben had seen plenty of dead people, but if they had nice faces, and this chap had had a nice face if a bit stern like, and if they hadn't died natural, it upset him.

''E may 'ave a wife or a kid,' thought Ben. 'I'll find aht wot Mr Smith's gime is, and I'll see 'e swings fer it!'

Having come to which decision, Ben felt a little better. Okay! That was settled, then. Next?

The next thing was to get up, see if his legs would obey him, and if by some miracle they would, use them to tour the premises and to find the larder.

Cautiously he raised himself to a sitting position and steered himself round and off the bed. To his surprise he did not topple, and after a moment or two he took a few steps. These proved that he was weak all right, but he could manage. Jest tike it easy, and yer can manidge.

He began to walk round the room. Its atmosphere of gloom was accentuated by the fact that the daylight was beginning to fade outside, and suddenly realising this he looked about anxiously for an electric light switch or a lamp. He saw neither. On the mantelpiece were a couple of candles in worn metal candlesticks. Well, they were better than nothing, though candles made nasty shadows; and the sight of a box of matches by one of the candlesticks brought back a little of Ben's fading comfort.

Over the mantelpiece was the replaced mirror. As Ben drew up to it, he received a shock. Lummy, 'oo was this bloke lookin' at 'im orf the wall? Then he remembered that it was his other self, and he glared at it. His other self glared back.

'Wot am I goin' ter do with yer, Marmerduke?' he demanded. 'I don't know you and yer don't know me, but if we carn't git away from each other I expeck we'll 'ave ter chum up some'ow, won't we? I wish yer could jest see yerself—yer looks like Gawd knows wot!'

Refraining from lighting a candle, for artificial lighting was not necessary just yet and if these were the only two he was destined to find he must not waste wax, he continued his tour of the room. It was a shabby incomplete affair. Bed, couple of chairs, a chest of drawers with three knobs missing, a small table that wobbled if you touched it, a cheap faded carpet, and no washstand. Why did he notice that there was no washstand? He always got along quite well without them.

'That must be you, Marmerduke,' he said. 'You washes!'

It began to dawn on him that Marmaduke had his uses. He was at least somebody to talk to. Ben spoke to him again when he reached the window.

'Lummy, there's a view fer sore eyes!' he exclaimed. 'Bomb site, eh? Wot a mess!'

It was indeed a depressing view. At the back of the house, it comprised a large square walled space which enclosed a scattered conglomeration of dead buildings on torn ground. The ground was untidy with debris and full of holes. The buildings were most of them scarred beyond repair, but one or two looked sound, notably one low brick structure that stretched to the back wall of the house, just below where Ben was peering. A black cat was sitting on the roof. Suddenly it swooped away.

'See that, Marmerduke?' said Ben. ''E's 'ad enuf! So've I!'

He turned away from the window, and now taking one of the candlesticks and the box of matches in case he needed them, he adventured farther afield. The wooden landing outside the bedroom was uncarpeted, and so were the stairs that invited Ben grimly down to the next floor, but before accepting the invitation he poked his head into another room on the floor he was on, and found it completely empty.

Now he began to descend the stairs. The stained wallpaper was peeling off the walls, and one bit curled at him as he passed it and touched his nose. He decided not to go quite so fast. He made a breeze.

The next floor was more spacious, though definitely not palatial, and there were four rooms, a cupboard, and a bathroom. Three of the rooms were empty, the other had a bed, a stool and a disconnected gas fire. The gas fire stood in the centre of the floor and looked self-conscious and unhappy. The floor was uncarpeted. There was a damp patch in one corner which Ben hoped was water, but he did not investigate. The bathroom had a rusty yellow bathtub with two taps, only one of which would turn on. The cupboard had a broom that swooped out at Ben and shot him back in one bound to the head of the next staircase.

''Ow I 'ates cubberds,' he muttered. 'When I 'ave my 'ouse built there won't be none!'

Halfway down the next flight he paused at a thought.

'Did Mr Smith and 'is friend cart me up orl these stairs? They'd of saived a bit o' work if they'd kep' me at the bottom! Barmy, Marmerduke, wern't they?'

At the bottom he found himself on the ground floor, and a sense of disappointment pervaded him when he noticed that still further stairs led to a basement. As with cupboards, so with basements; none would figure in Ben's dream house. The hall was wide, and the rooms opening into it were larger than those on the upper floors, but again only one had any furniture in it—a back room the window of which looked on to the roof where the cat had sat. There was a couch in this room which almost suggested comfort. So did an armchair. This appearance may have been partly due to the fact that they stood on the best carpet Ben had so far come across, but a gate-legged table with a blue china vase upon it helped, and so did a bookcase in a corner. If there were no flowers in the vase or books in the bookcase, these omissions did not entirely destroy the comparative homeliness of these two items. The window overlooking the view of the low roof had long maroon curtains, now half-drawn . . . Something funny about that roof. What was it? Just it being so low? Couldn't be more than four or five feet of headroom, you'd think. Wunner wot it had been used for? Wot abart a squint?

But when Ben began to draw the long maroon curtain more aside, his mind was abruptly switched away from the roof and he forgot all about it. Behind the bottom of the curtain was another vase, broken into four pieces, and as he had disarranged the curtain's folds one of the pieces had come rolling out. Something else also slid across the little space of polished boards between the wall and the edge of the carpet. A hammer.

'Narsty,' thought Ben.

Then he rounded on himself.

'Why is it narsty?' he demanded, aloud. 'Anybody can break a vase, carn't they, Marmerduke?'

It was on the hammer, however, that his eyes were riveted as he spoke. Suddenly, against his will, he bent down to get a closer view of the part you hit with. Some little threads were sticking to it. It wouldn't be hair—would it?

He turned and left the room. The hall seemed to have grown immeasurably darker during the short time that had elapsed since he had left it. He did not stop walking until he had reached the front door. He wanted to get as far away from that hammer as he could.

He found himself opening the front door. He could not have said just why he was doing it. He had not made any conscious decision to leave, for he had worked all that out already; and a hammer with hair on it was merely one small incident in a series of which the beginning was a back with a knife in it. Probably it was because he needed a bit of air. Yes, that must be it. The air that came at him as he stood in the doorway was cool and refreshing. Nice. Sort of eased down your prickles. And where he stood was midway between outside and inside, without actually being in either. Wouldn't mind staying here for ever!

His momentary contentment did not last. In Ben's experience contentment rarely did. It was ended by two eyes gleaming at him out of the gloaming, and he could not readjust his focus swiftly enough to make out at once whether the eyes were just before him or across the street. Were they Mr Smith's eyes, and was he standing on the opposite pavement, watching? No, they weren't Mr Smith's eyes. You'd hardly spot them so clearly all that distance, and besides, *his* eyes weren't green . . .

The eyes loomed suddenly closer, and a dark sleek body flashed past him into the house. He flashed back after it, closed the door, and sat down on the ground. Now facing him again, and purring hard, sat the black cat he had first seen on the low roof at the back.

'Nah, listen,' said Ben, seriously. 'I don't mind cats, pertickler if they're strays, so I'll fergive yer this time—but any more dirty tricks like that, and aht yer go! Got that, Sammy? Okay! Then come along and keep me company dahn in the bisement.'

The basement looked completely dark as he stood at the top of the final flight, and he decided that this time he would need his candle. He lit it first match, which is pretty good when your hand isn't steady; and now the shadows he so cordially detested began. What he couldn't understand, as his own shadow wobbled and shifted around him, was what use they were. Light, okay, but why shadders?

And why stone steps? All the others had been wood. Of course, some wooden stairs creaked, and plenty had creaked up above, but once you knew which ones they were you could give 'em a miss, and they didn't go clang-clang like these stone ones were doing. Lummy, he sounded like the whole British Army!

Sammy, on the other hand, slithered down ahead of him without a sound.

And now began the most unpleasant part of the whole unpleasant tour. With no light beyond that of the flickering candle, and with his shadow—or, rather, Marmaduke's—now darting all over the place as its unwilling owner jerked his way from spot to spot, poked his head in doorways, and swung round at every sound, real or imagined, Ben checked up on the kitchen and scullery and larder (a bit

41

disappointing, the larder, but it contained enough to go on with) and cupboards. In the scullery he found the beetle population, and left them hurriedly in control.

''Ow abart you 'avin' a go at 'em, Sammy?' he suggested, before he closed the door.

But Sammy, with tail up, refused to take on the job.

All this while Ben had been anticipating the locked door, wondering whether he was ever coming to it, and he was beginning to believe that Mr Smith had invented it to frighten him when suddenly he found it before him. It was the very last door he had tried in the basement, along a narrow passage at the back that led to nowhere else. He thought it was just another cupboard, for he did not imagine that the basement space allowed for any more rooms, but the fact that it was locked suggested that it must be the room to which Mr Smith had referred. Ben gazed at it speculatively.

'Wot's on the other side, Sammy?' he asked the cat at his strangely polished feet. As the cat made no response, he passed the enquiry on to the third of the party. 'Orl right, let's 'ear wot *you've* gotter say, Marmerduke? Wot's in that there room? Storidge, 'e sed. Orl right, then. Wot's bein' stored?'

In the most refined voice Ben could muster—it was a pity the performance was wasted on a cat—Marmaduke replied:

'Glass and silvah, wot?'

'That's ain't a bad idea o' yourn, Marmerduke,' agreed Ben, 'and p'r'aps they locked it up 'cos that other caretaiker 'ad a go at it? That would explain why they got rid of 'im.'

But somehow Ben did not believe that was the true reason.

'And then they'd lock that in a cupboard, wouldn't they? Not in a room?'

''Ow dew yew know it is not a cubbard, wot?' answered Marmerduke.

''Cos 'e sed the locked door was the door of a room,' Ben retorted. 'Put that in yer side-whiskers and smoke it!'

'Dew yew believe awl 'e sed?' enquired Marmaduke, in no way perturbed.

'No, I don't, and that's a fack,' agreed Ben, 'but nah yer can keep yer trap shut 'cos I've 'ad enuff o' yer.'

He turned to go, for the larder called, but all at once he turned back, realising that he had omitted an obvious effort to get a glimpse of what the room contained. He put his eye to the key-hole.

At first he saw nothing but blackness. He thought this was due to a key on the other side, but the test of a matchstick disproved this theory, for the match went in the little aperture too fast and before he realised it he found that he had posted it. Lummy, wot a waste! He might need that match before he'd finished here! Still, it was gone, and there was no getting it back, so he'd just have one more squint, and then . . .

He kept his eye at the key-hole longer this time. Sometimes, when there's no intruding key, the eye becomes acclimatised, and gradually things become a bit clearer. Yes, and weren't they doing it now? Not much clearer, but just a bit. Wasn't that the back of a chair? No. Yes. Well, might be. And wasn't there a sort of shape beyond? Like a—like a—wot? It wouldn't be a stacher, would it? Ben didn't like stachers. If you looked at 'em too long you expected them to move! Gawd! This 'un was movin'!

A sudden ray of light, as from a torch, illuminated for

an instant the floor at the moving statue's feet. Then the ray went out. Ben tried not to feel sick. In that momentary shaft of light he had seen what lay on the other side of the door. It lay on the floor motionless, with arms outstretched.

6

Very Brief Respite

No one, and Ben least of all, could have called Ben a brave man. 'Some'ow I seems ter git through,' he would have told you, 'but it ain't through not bein' a cowwid, yer carn't 'elp 'ow yer was born, well, can yer?' The two kinds of people he admired most of all in this difficult world were those who could twirl china plates in opposite directions on the tips of billiard cues and those who stood firm before corpses.

Of course, sometimes you stood firm because the corpses mezzermised you and took away yer legs like. That kind of standing firm didn't count. In fact, it truly was not standing firm at all, because since you usually ended on the floor you'd be more accurate to call it sitting plonk.

Now Ben sat plonk.

But he only sat for an instant. This was due to the circumstance that he sat plonk on the cat, which so upset them both that before either of them realised it they were both pelting up the basement stairs in sympathetic unison.

The cat's panic was again soundless, but Ben's boots on the cold stone clanked more loudly than ever. This time it was the British Army in retreat.

Was the moving statue behind the locked door, now growing blessedly more and more distant, hearing the retreat? ''Ow fur,' wondered Ben, for you can still think in a sort of a way while you run, ''ow fur does boots on stairs 'ave ter be from a door not ter be 'eard on t'other side?' In the absence of definite knowledge, the only logical plan is to make it as fur as possible.

And as fur as possible, of course, was the top room from which Ben had started.

He and Sammy reached it in a dead heat. Lurching into the room which had once seemed a prison but which now seemed a sanctuary, Ben tottered to the bed and sank down on it. Sammy leapt beside him, and for a few seconds they comforted each other. Then, when speech became possible, Ben spoke to his companion.

'Sammy,' he said. 'You and me's friends. Once I shot a cat. Corse, not with a real gun, it was one o' them hair-guns, and I didn't mean ter 'it it, but I was never good at shootin', and when I tries ter 'it a thing I misses and when I tries ter miss a thing, I 'its, and so I 'it that cat. And I wancher ter know I'm sorry.'

In some things, if not many, Ben was an optimist, and he convinced himself that Sammy understood.

But one couldn't just go on lying and talking to a cat, so after a little while Ben sat up and tried to become practical again. He had not yet paid that return visit to the larder, most unfortunately located in the basement, and his stomach would have no chance of returning to normal until he got something inside it. Before making another descent, however, he had to do a little constructive thinking. He thought aloud, to Sammy.

'There's more'n us two in the 'ouse,' he said. 'I mean, us three, 'cos we carn't leave aht Marmerduke. 'Ow are yer, Marmerduke? I ain't seed yer laitely, but if I went acrorst ter that lookin'-glass I'd find yer was still 'ere! Yus, but besides us three, there's a fourth in the room with the locked door, the one wot we calls the Stacher. 'E's got a torch. Wot else 'as 'e got? Wot we're 'opin', ain't we, Sammy and Marmerduke, is that 'e ain't got a gun. *Or* a key! We don't want 'im poppin' aht on us, do we? Yus, but p'r'aps 'e ain't got a key? P'r'aps 'e's a prisoner like, bein' kep' locked up? Yus, 'ow abart that?'

Not precisely an exhilarating thought, yet there was some comfort in it.

Turning then from the living to the dead, Ben continued his reflections, while the black cat beside him concentrated on licking its paws smooth.

'Nah, then. 'Ow abart that corpse? It mikes a cupple, one ahtside on a seat, one inside on the floor. Yus, that bloke on the floor was a deader, no mistike abart it. Bein' dead ain't like bein' asleep. When yer see a deader there's somethink abart 'em that tells yer they ain't never comin' back. Corse, I on'y seed 'im fer a momint when the torch went on 'im. We didn't waite fer no more, did we, Sammy? Yer ain't listenin'! Go on, chuck yer paws, they're orl right, and listen, wot I'm sayin' is important. See, nah, Sammy, I'm *comin'* ter it! I'm comin' ter the 'orrerble thort! 'Oo is the corpse? 'Ave *you* any idea?'

Apparently Sammy had none.

'Well, 'ow abart you, Marmerduke? Wot's goin' on atween *your* side-whiskers?'

But Marmaduke proved as barren as the cat.

'A lot o' good you are, the pair of yer!' said Ben, disgustedly. But it was nice talking to them, just the same. Not only for the companionship of one's voice, but also because it gave one a sort of superior feeling. After all, however lowly you are, you're a cut above a cat and a feller wot ain't. 'Orl right, I'll tell yer 'oo *I* think 'e might be. Git ready, 'cos this ain't goin' ter be nice. 'Ow abart 'im bein' the larst caretaiker? . . . Lummy! . . . See, I'm the nex'!'

Ben rather wished he had not mentioned this thought aloud. It seemed to fix it like. For comfort he added, rather hastily,

'Corse, it's on'y an idea, minjer. I may be wrong!'

But he felt uncomfortably sure that he was not wrong. And, even if he were, the man had been dead, hadn't he? No doubt whatever about that.

Well, there it was, and when he tried to think beyond this he found that he could not. He had come up against a wall in his mind, and partly because it was a very tired mind existing precariously above a very empty stomach, he had to give up any further mental effort. And don't forget, he excused himself, he'd had a dose of something put inside him not so long ago, and that never did nobody no good, did it?

'So I'm goin' dahn ter git me supper, Sammy,' he said. 'Jest that, and nothink else. And this time yer'd better stay 'ere and waite fer me. See, if I gits any more shocks I don't wanter sit dahn on yer agine.'

Sammy, now with green eyes closed, agreed. The cat was far too comfortable to evince any desire to move.

So down Ben went again, putting blinkers on his thoughts,

and kept resolutely moving until he found himself once more in the larder.

For twenty minutes life became bearable again. In the bread-bin he found three-quarters of a loaf of bread. One of those nice, easy loaves, with the slices already cut for you. Slices a bit thin, perhaps, for the ideal conception, but if you lumped a couple of thin ones together, that made one thick one. And there was a tin of shrimp paste to use between as glue. The shrimp paste was all right underneath, once you'd scraped off the top layer of green. Then there were two tins of sardines, and one tin of Heinz's Cooked Spaghetti in Tomato Sauce with Cheese, and one of Heinz's Cooked Macaroni in Cream Sauce with Cheese. Big 'uns, both. In spite of the cheese, Ben decided on the sardines, because you were supposed to eat sardines cold while Heinz needed to be warmed, and he didn't want to waste time trying to do any cooking. Tin-opener? Gawd! Suppose there wasn't one? He searched in a panic, but found the precious implement at last in a drawer in the kitchen table, and opening one of the sardine tins he feasted first his eyes, and then his stomach, on six fat oily little darlings. He ate them straight out of the tin, skin, backbone, oil and all. Saved washin' up. And, spotting a bottle of Yorkshire Relish after he had got half-way through the contents of the tin, he filled it up again with the sauce, and for two glorious if somewhat startling minutes lived in heaven.

'It mikes yer sweat,' he admitted, when he had licked the tin clean, 'but, lummy, it's good!'

What happened next was not quite so good. The front-door bell rang.

7

Conversation on a Doorstep

Ben's first feeling on hearing the bell was one of resentment. Wasn't he ever to be let alone? This was what he had meant to safeguard himself against when he had tried to get Mr Smith to define and limit his working hours.

If the person who had rung the front-door bell was a house-hunter, this was a most unreasonable time to call! How can you expect to see a house properly if you're shown over it by candle-light? On the other hand, if the person were not a house-hunter, then there would probably be other good reasons against answering this late summons.

'They'll 'ave ter ring twice,' decided Ben, 'if they're goin' ter git me!'

They did ring twice, and the second ring was followed by the sound of the door-knocker. Lummy, he s'posed he'd have to go! But if he had any say in the matter, which was of course a moot point, he did not intend to make himself pleasant.

Managing to keep his eyes from straying along the passage towards the room with the locked door—he was trying hard not to think of that—he left the kitchen and mounted the basement stairs, candle held before him, his shadow sliding up behind. When he reached the hall he was tempted to desert his duty and to continue mounting up to the top, but he knew that the candle-light would be betraying its flickering presence in the fanlight above the front door, so he could not pretend that nobody was in the house. Taking a deep breath—it sort of steadied him like—he went to the door, transferred the candlestick from his right hand to his left, grasped the door-knob, paused, then turned the knob quickly and pulled the door open.

His action was so sudden that the feeble flame of the candle failed to survive the draught of air that came through the doorway, and went out. There was no unkind trick that had not been played on Ben in moments of tenseness. He had had even this one before. The dim figure standing before him on the doorstep might be anybody from the Archbishop of Canterbury to a devil with a forked tail. The voice that addressed him, however, clearly came from neither.

'Perhaps if you relit it,' said the voice, 'we could see each other.'

It was a woman's voice. Apart from a certain strained tenseness in it, it was not unpleasant. Feeling that, so far, things were not as bad as they might have been, and might soon become, Ben fumbled for his matches. Then it occurred to him that after all there might be some advantage in darkness, and it would be as well to delay lighting up.

"Oojer want?' he asked.

'I prefer to see who I'm talking to,' came the response.

'Oh! But if yer've come ter the wrong 'ouse—'

'Isn't this Number 19?'

'Well, yus.'

'Billiter Road?'

That destroyed his happy hope.

'That's right,' he answered. 'But it's a bit laite fer callin', ain't it?'

'If it were earlier,' replied the woman, 'we would not need that candle to talk by. Aren't you going to light it?'

He supposed he would have to, and he did so with an inward sigh. He struck a match, applied it to the wick, and the little flame glowed again. By its insufficient illumination Ben saw that the woman was young and rather attractive, if not exactly his meat. He preferred 'em plump and fair, and this 'un was dark and slim. Nice neat dress, anyhow. In fact, you shouldn't call her a woman, really. She was a lidy.

All at once Ben switched off her on to himself. He stopped thinking of what he was looking at and thought of what she was looking at, and a wave of self-consciousness swept over him. This was the first person, not counting his employer, who had seen him in his new guise, and quite apart from getting used to being seen like he wasn't, it set up a pretty problem. Should he try and talk like he thought Marmaduke would, or go on being natural like? His natural voice certainly did not fit his neat attire. A cat as audience didn't matter, but this was a very different cup o' tea.

'Thank you, that's better,' said the young lady.

'Don't menshun,' returned Ben.

'Then I won't.' There was something odd in her voice, a hardness which somehow Ben did not think natural. Was she playing a part, too? But Ben did not quite believe that, either. Probably there was some other reason, and not a nice one. 'May I know who you are?'

Another poser! Ben wasn't sure himself.

'My nime's Jones,' he stated, 'if that's anythink, thing, to yer.'

'No—I don't think we've met.' Yus, something very odd about that voice. For all its hardness and confidence, was she so sure of herself, after all? She was thinkin' 'ard—yer could tell that. 'You live here, don't you?'

That was a funny question. You call at a house, some-body opens the door, and you ask if he lives there!

'Well, that's right,' agreed Ben, watchfully.

'Alone?'

Should he admit it? And—was he alone? Lummy, what *did* she want? Obviously she was not a house-hunter.

'Well, that's one way o' puttin' it,' he replied.

'Oh! And what would be another way of putting it?'

This wasn't any good! He was getting in a tangle. He tried to untangle himself.

'Wot I means, miss,' he said, 'is I ain't the owner of this 'ouse.'

He found her looking at him curiously, and a little more closely.

'No—I suppose not. One of the—staff, I suppose?'

'Well, I answers the bell.'

'Of course. How stupid of me. You would be the man-servant here. Tell me, you've answered the bell to—to—' Her voice wavered, then suddenly it grew firm again. 'You've answered the bell to a Mr Bretherton, haven't you?'

Mr Bretherton? What did he say to that?

'Haven't you?' she repeated, sharply.

Bretherton. Now who was Bretherton? Would that be Mr Smith's pal? Or—lummy!—the statue? Or, come to that, was the statue the pal? Or would it be the bloke on the floor, sayin' 'e was the larst caretaiker—or even sayin' 'e wasn't? . . .

'What's the matter with you!' exclaimed the young lady.

''Arf a mo'—I got a toothache,' muttered Ben, trying to get back. 'See, miss, yer got it a bit wrong. I'm the caretaiker o' this 'ouse, and it's ter be sold, see, and, well, all I does is ter answer the bell and let people go over the plice. It's a bit laite, so I don't s'pose you've come to go over it? 'Ave yer?'

Now *she* seemed a little lost for an answer. It was a nice exchange.

'And, any'ow,' went on Ben, pressing his advantage, 'I ain't supposed ter show nobody over not withaht they come from Waivell and Son—'

He stopped abruptly as a spasm flashed across her face. Or was it just the candle flickering? A few seconds went by without either of them speaking. Then she said, in a low voice:

'Yes, of course. Wavell and Son. Yes. It would have been from Wavell and Son that Mr Bretherton would have come here. Are you sure you don't remember the name?'

'Afraid not, miss,' replied Ben.

'Perhaps he didn't give his name? You may recognise a description? Rather tall—'

'Brahn 'air, and a small brahn mustache?'

'No!'

Then it wasn't Mr Smith. For a moment Ben had thought it might be.

'Greyish hair,' the lady went on, 'though I don't mean

he was old. He hadn't any moustache, he was clean shaven. Rather a—well, solemn looking man, with a rather quick, abrupt way of speaking—' She paused, with a little helpless shrug. 'I'm afraid that doesn't tell you much.'

'It don't tell me nothink,' answered Ben, 'and any'ow I wouldn't of seed 'im even if 'e 'ad called.'

'Why not? Didn't you say you were the caretaker here?'

'Yus, but I was on'y took on this arternoon, and you're the fust person wot's called since I took on the job.'

The lady frowned disappointedly.

'I see. Then, of course—he may have been here, only you wouldn't—'

Her voice trailed off. She seemed to have come to a dead end. Taking her eyes from Ben's face, she looked beyond him into the hall, as though trying to pierce its dimness. Then her eyes returned to Ben.

'So you can't help me,' she said.

Her voice was no longer hard. All at once Ben found himself wishing he could help her.

'P'r'aps if yer told me a bit more,' he suggested, 'I might be able ter?'

An odd moment followed. She looked at him with a new expression, a puzzled expression. Then the faintest smile came, so faint that in the candle-light you could hardly see it.

'One of your side-whiskers is coming off,' she said.

'Gawd!' gasped Ben, and then blushed at the giveaway.

'You think side-whiskers suit you, perhaps?' she asked.

'See, it was like this,' he answered, struggling to recover his lost ground. 'I allus wears 'em, but this mornin' I shaved one orf by mistake like, so I 'ad to stick another on ter fit the one I still 'ad.'

'I see. When you applied for this job. That is the most delightful lie I have ever heard. You don't really expect me to believe you, do you?'

'Yer can do as yer like abart that.'

'Thank you, I will. You mentioned a man with a moustache.'

'Did I?'

'Who is he?'

'Eh? Oh, jest some'un, miss. Yer wouldn't know 'im.'

'Did he engage you?'

'Well, s'pose 'e did?'

'I'm asking you.'

'Yus, but might *I* arsk why?'

She drew a little closer to him. She was prettier than he had thought. Yes, but what was the use of dwelling on that if you hadn't been born a toff?

'I thought you were willing to help me?' she said.

'Yus, but yer've fergot somethink,' he reminded her. 'I sed if yer told me a bit more.'

She hesitated, and suddenly twisted her head round to glance at the dark street behind her. Some way up the street was a lamp post, but the light only reached the vicinity of No. 19 as the faintest glow.

'What more do you want to be told?' she asked, turning back to him.

'Well, I wanter know why yer wanter know, like I sed,' he replied. 'And then, this 'ere Mr Bretherton? I ain't 'eard yet 'oo *'e* is, or why yer wanter find aht if 'e's bin 'ere?' He took a risk. "Ow abart comin' in fer a minit? There's one o' the rooms we could tork in. That is, yer know, if—'

Footsteps came along the street, and as they drew closer panic seemed to seize her.

'Not now—later!' she whispered.

And the next moment she was gone.

Panic is catching. Ben quickly closed the door. The approaching footsteps drew up to the house, ceased for a few seconds, and then continued on again.

8

The Thing

This time Ben did not return straight to his bedroom. He stopped at the floor below, went into the bathroom, and put his head under the cold tap. The water came out yellow. He had a vague recollection of a towel somewhere in the bedroom, but as he could not wait for it and there was no towel here, he gave his dripping wig a preliminary dry on a soiled window-curtain, and then mounted to his room to complete the job. He had to turn the cat off the towel to do it.

'Yer know, yer orter leave my things alone, Sammy,' he remonstrated, dwelling for the moment on minor troubles in order to postpone the contemplation of major ones. 'That towel was put there fer Marmerduke, not fer you. Cats don't need no towels—they jest licks theirselves and leaves the dryin' ter nacher.'

The reference to Marmaduke took him to the mirror to see whether ablutions had washed away any of his second self. He discovered that Marmaduke was still all there—materially, if not quite mentally—saving for the disarrangement of one side-whisker, and it was while he was working it back into position that his mind reverted to the lady who had first drawn his attention to the side-whisker's inclination to stray. He sighed on to the mirror, blotting Marmaduke out with his breath. There was something in a good sigh, after all.

'*Now* 'ow many 'ave we got?' he communed. 'Feller dead on a seat. Another feller dead on a floor. A movin' stacher. Me, Gawd knows 'oo. And, laitest, a lidy on a doorstep wot bunks when she 'ears footsteps.'

But who had indicated, he recalled as he remembered her last words, that she would be coming back again.

'Oh, and jest one more, fer fun. 'Oo's the footsteps?'

A sudden yearning for sleep seized him. Not because he was tired, though he was, but because sleep blots out all. He moved towards the bed in which he had awakened from his last slumber. That was a very different slumber from the slumber he hoped for now. It had been forced, and he had been deposited on the bed. This sleep would be natural—he yawned, to make sure of it—and he would get on the bed by his own decision.

Sammy was momentarily in possession. Why it had temporarily left the bed's comfort for a towel in a corner was beyond Ben's reasoning, not fitted to cope with feline logic, but as it seemed a shame to keep on disturbing it, he decided there was room for two.

The next thing to decide was whether to take off any clothes. There were not, as a rule, many to take off, but it was Marmaduke going to bed this time, not Ben, and there was no knowing how much Marmaduke had on underneath. It might be interesting to explore? On the other hand, if he took them off tonight he would only have to put them on again tomorrow. So he let them stay.

Lying beside his unusual bed-companion, Ben closed his eyes and tried to sleep, but when he found himself drifting into a museum filled with statues armed with bread-knives he opened his eyes and tried to keep awake. This was not fair! Sleep should come first, and the dreams or nightmares afterwards.

Presently he tried again. Ah, this was better! Now he was floating on a dark quiet river. Nice, this was. He hoped he'd go on floating like this for ever. P'r'aps this was what you did in heaven? Jest float! But then, of course, it wasn't likely that chaps like Ben would ever get to heaven. Well, was it? And, even if he did get there, he'd prefer the river a bit wider than this one—in fact, more of a sea, like—because he was a bit too near the bank, and he could hear something walking along the bank with a sort of a scrunch-scrunch. What would it be? A cow? Yes, p'r'aps a cow. Some animal, anyway. At least . . . would it be an animal? Crunch-crunch. It—it couldn't be a person, could it? Or—a stacher? Lummy! He tried to stop floating so the Thing by his side would get ahead of him. It took an awful effort. You had to clench your teeth and curl your toes. But—thank Gawd!—at last he did it! He had stopped moving . . .

A moment later he realised, with a sinking heart, that he had thanked God too soon. He had certainly stopped, but so had the Thing beside him! In vain he listened for the crunch-crunch of steps fading away in the distance. He strained his ears till they nearly burst. He could not hear whatever stood so near him, he could not see it, but he knew it was there. He felt its presence, pinning him to the spot where he lay, and it was looking down on him. An effort to start floating again proved abortive. You cannot float on a river that is no longer there; and you cannot float on a bed.

If he had been asked how long he lay there with eyes tightly closed, pinned down by an unseen presence and waiting for something to happen without the least idea what, he could have given no answer. It might have been five seconds or five minutes. But when at last he could stand it no longer and was forced to put an end to his ignorance by opening his eyes, he saw only darkness. Not the utter darkness that tells you nothing. It was a darkness faintly alleviated by a percolating dimness which would have revealed any looming shape beside the bed had it been present.

Ben was perfectly certain it had been present. And suddenly he heard the sound which earlier he would have welcomed. Crunch-crunch. In the passage. And gradually fading away down the stairs. Whoever or whatever was responsible for those sounds had left the bedside before he had opened his eyes, and had been waiting outside the door until this moment.

Fear can hold you still or set you in movement. Now it set Ben in movement, for he felt he had to know what the Thing was that had entered his nightmare and then continued outside it. He rolled off the bed, picked himself up from the floor, made for the door, then changed his direction and ran to the mantelpiece. He was going down, but not without a candle. When the little flame had glowed to its full dimensions he received another small shock. The cat was no longer on the bed. Was the Thing the cat? He quickly dismissed the absurd idea, for no cat could make such sounds unless it had swelled to fantastic size! He tried to call to it, but no words came. His throat had gone on strike.

Now he was out in the passage, the candle held high. That was the way to reduce the shadows, and a shadow is no man's friend. But you can't hold a candle up aloft all the time, and half-way down the stairs his arm came down, and his shadow shivered beside him along the wall. 'Go on, am I wobblin' like that?' he thought. He hoped it was due to the flickering flame.

No sign of anything, or anyone. Aside from himself and his black counterpart. Down one flight. A swift glance along the landing towards the bathroom. Down another flight. Still nothing. No—half a mo'! Wasn't that a sound on the basement stairs?

He hesitated, moved towards the head of the final flight, then paused again. Something was happening behind him. Lummy! What?

Sandwiched between two evils, he chose the one behind him, and turned. The fanlight above the door, which usually only showed faintly at this time, now glowed clearly, its crescent shape defined. The glow vanished—came again—vanished again. Then history repeated itself, and someone knocked on the door.

9

Caller No. Two

Well, there was no use hesitating. Once a door 'got at you,' as Ben expressed it, it wouldn't let you alone and it had to be opened. So better get it over!

But as he opened the door an idea occurred to him that comforted his jangled nerves. It would be the lady, of course! She had intimated that she was coming back, and probably she had been hanging around somewhere or other waiting till she could be certain that the coast was clear. It would be all right if it was her. She was a nice lady, the only visitor he wouldn't mind opening the door to. Only of course he'd have to see that she didn't come to any harm. 'If this ain't no 'ealth cure fer me,' he reflected, 'neither it ain't fer 'er.'

His guess proved wrong. He did not find the lady standing in the porch. He found a policeman.

The unwelcome constable flashed his torch in Ben's face for a moment, nearly blinding him, and then spoke. His voice was amiable enough.

'Up late, aren't you?' he said.

'Well, 'oo's got me up?' retorted Ben.

'Oh! Were you in bed?'

'Eh?'

'If so, it didn't take you long to change out of your pyjamas.'

'I don't wear perjarmers.'

'P'r'aps not, but do you sleep in your clothes?'

'Nah, listen, copper,' answered Ben. 'Yer sed it was laite yerself, and if yer've called ter tork abart me clothes yer can 'op it, and come back in the mornin'. See, I ain't 'avin' any!'

The policeman refused to oblige. Instead of hopping it he advanced a step closer.

'I haven't come to talk about your clothes,' he said, 'I've come to talk about something a bit more serious.'

'Wot's that?'

'You couldn't guess, I suppose?'

'This ain't "Twenty Questions"!'

'Meaning by that you have no idea why I'm here?'

'I'll know when yer tells me.'

'Right, sonny! Have it your own way. I've called in reference to a murder, and you can tell me whether you know anything about it. Mind if I step inside?'

Without waiting for permission the constable stepped inside, and then closed the door behind him.

Ben thought hard, but nothing came. This was grievous, for he was up against a moment of decision. Should he fence with the law, or throw himself upon its mercy? The question ran uselessly round and round his mind. It ran alone, without the answer. Meanwhile, after a short silence during which the policeman glanced along the hall towards the top of the basement stairs, Ben found another question shot at him.

'Are you all by yourself in the house?'

That wasn't an easy one, either. In the first place, he didn't know. Was he or wasn't he? And even if he did know, and it was one or the other, should he tell? Of course, you couldn't count a cat, and he didn't suppose the constable would reckon Ben and Marmaduke as two. At this thought Ben suddenly recalled that the constable was viewing Marmaduke, and made a note of it. But beyond and transcending the cat and his second self, there were the Stacher and the Thing . . .

'What's up with you?'

'Eh?'

'Gone dumb or something?'

'I'm torkin', ain't I?'

'Well, go on talking. I asked if you were alone here in the house?'

'Alone, eh?'

'That's what I said. Never heard the word before?'

'Well, yer don't see nobody else, do yer?'

'That's a fact, but when the door-bell rings, does the whole family come along to answer it?'

'Well, I ain't got no famerly.'

'I can't believe it!'

'Wot, that I got no famerly?'

'No, that you've actually told me something! Watch that candle, the grease is spilling. How about going into a room and sitting down? And putting that candle down on a table?'

But as the policeman moved towards one of the doors Ben realised that it might be a good idea to assert himself. Even with a policeman—perhaps particularly with a policeman—you needed to keep your end up until they got bang on top of you.

'Oi! 'Arf a mo'!' he exclaimed.

'Arf a mo'? There was rather too much of Ben in that, and not quite enough of Marmaduke!

'Jest a minit, if you don't mind,' he added. 'This 'ouse ain't—is not your'n, yer know!'

'I'm not sure that I'd want it,' replied the policeman, good-humouredly.

Of course you could never be sure of a bobby's good humour. You never knew what was going on underneath. Wink at you one moment, arrest you the next!

'Well, yer ain't got it! It berlongs ter the person wot I'm employed by, and I'm lookin' arter it!'

The policeman nodded.

'Good enough! Then how about sitting on the stairs and putting that candle on the floor? I don't suppose your employer would thank you if you burned his house down!'

He moved to the main staircase as he spoke, and sat down on the stair second from the bottom, his large legs wide apart. If Ben had sat down on the bottom stair between them his head wouldn't have come much higher than the policeman's stomach. He decided not to occupy the space. But he did put the candle on the floor, which shot the policeman's shadow half-way up the stairs and made him wish he hadn't. Somehow the policeman seemed to have grown several sizes larger.

'Who is your employer?' enquired the policeman, casually.

''Enery the Eighth.'

'Try again.'

'Why should I tell yer 'oo 'e is afore yer tells *me* why yer wanter know?'

'I see. You're one of the cautious ones, are you? Well,

we'll leave that for the moment, if you like. If there's nobody in the house but yourself—' The policeman paused, but Ben did not corroborate the statement. 'Then I suppose you'd be the caretaker?'

'Yer can call me that, if yer like.'

'Thank you. I will. And this house is to let?'

'That's right. Leastwise, no, it ain't.'

'Isn't it?'

'No, it's ter be sold.'

'Oh! Well, that's near enough, so now suppose we get down to business?'

'Ain't I waitin' fer it?'

'You won't have to wait any longer. I've already told you what I've come about, so you'll be wise now to answer my questions without any more nonsense!'

A point of law occurred to Ben. He was not an expert in legal procedure, but he did know a bit about policemen.

'Do I 'ave ter?' he enquired.

The constable regarded him thoughtfully for a moment, then smiled.

'Wise as well as cautious, eh?' he said. 'Well, shall we put it this way, sonny? If you don't have to, you will be sensible to. If there's a next time, you may not then have the option! So now, then. Have you had any callers lately?'

'Wot sort o' callers?'

'Any sort. House-hunters, for instance?'

'No.'

'Anybody else?'

'Wot?'

'Suppose we cut out the "wot's"'

'Well, 'oo else would there be?'

The constable did not answer at once. He was looking

at Ben hard, while Ben was thinking hard. 'I gotter mike up me mind,' ran Ben's thinking. 'This is a charnce ter come aht with the 'ole thing, I mightn't git another, and there's a dead bloke dahn below, and that there Stacher chap. But if I starts, 'ow is 'e goin' ter tike it? Is 'e goin' ter believe me? And 'ow do I stand if 'e don't? Orf ter the staishun fer more questions, and me fingerprints on the knife, would they let me go agine, and if I wasn't 'ere nex' time Smith comes along 'e'll smell a rat, and 'e won't give nothink away that's goin' ter 'urt 'im nex' time the pleece come 'ere, 'e'll 'ave bin warned like, and 'e'll jest tell 'em I come along disguised arter the murder and must 'ave took the job ter 'ide meself, and they'll berlieve 'im and not me, and 'e'll git orf and I won't, but if I sticks 'ere meself I might catch 'im like 'e deserves, and then wot abart the lidy?' Funny how the lady stuck in his mind. 'She may need a bit of 'elp, and 'ow am I goin' ter 'elp 'er if I ain't 'ere?' Were these arguments sound? Was this just wishful thinking? Wishful thinking! Not that staying on here was any bed of roses! His mind wobbled and wavered. 'I dunno! P'r'aps it'd be best orl rahnd ter come aht with it. Yer can on'y die once. Yus, p'r'aps I'd better 'ave a shot at the truth, and if 'e berlieves me 'e'll know better'n me 'ow ter go abart things—'

One of the constable's hands was in a pocket.

'Maybe this will help you to answer me,' he said.

Lummy! Was he going to bring out a gun? What he brought out was not a gun, but it was equally unpleasant.

'Have a look at this,' ordered the constable. 'This is the person I'm interested in.'

Ben found himself gazing at a photograph of two men on a seat. One was himself. So Smith had done it! Had taken the photograph to the police! To Ben's astonishment, he kept his head.

'Wich 'un?' he asked.

'The one at the end where your thumb is,' replied the constable. 'The scarecrow.'

'Oh! And 'oo's the hother?'

'The man who was murdered.'

'Go on!'

'You don't know anything about it?'

''Ow should I?'

'Well, that's true enough. It only happened this afternoon.'

'Oh, did it?'

'And this picture won't be in the papers until tomorrow.'

'Oh! It's goin' in the paipers, is it?'

'You bet it is!'

''Oo give it to yer?'

'Oh, someone brought it along.'

'Yer mean—the bloke 'oo took it?'

'That's right.'

'Well, wot did 'e tike it for?'

'We might call it just an amateur's luck. He thought the two made an amusing picture, and never dreamt that he was photographing a murderer and his victim.'

'Oh! I see,' said Ben. 'The one wot yer calls the scarecrow is the one yer think did it?'

'The police certainly consider that possible,' answered the constable.

'But 'e mightn't of.'

'I don't expect it will be long before we prove it. You see, the knife had fingerprints on it.'

Ben's heart suddenly missed a beat. Not because the

knife had fingerprints on it. He already knew that. But so, now, had the photograph which the constable had handed to him. The prints of an exceedingly moist thumb and forefinger. But he still kept his head, albeit the head became moist, too, and he lowered the hand that held the photograph to his trouser-leg.

'What are you rubbing yourself for?' enquired the policeman.

'Got an itch,' answered Ben. 'This 'ouse is fair swarmin'. A knife, did yer say?'

'That's right.'

'Must 'ave mide a narsty mess!'

'It certainly did!'

'But I still ain't got it why yer've come 'ere?'

'I've told you. I want to know whether you've seen this fellow?'

'Corse not!'

'Quite sure?'

''Ow would I?'

'If he'd called.'

'Why would 'e call?'

'That's what I'd need to find out, if he had.'

'Well, 'e ain't,' said Ben, and suddenly added, 'Wot mikes yer think 'e might of?'

'No harm in letting you know that,' responded the policeman. 'I've been told he was seen entering this house.'

Ben stared. ''Oo told yer?' he demanded.

'That, if you don't mind,' returned the policeman, 'I will keep to myself.'

Of course Ben did not need any answer from the policeman. Only Smith could have been the informer, giving the information assumedly when he gave the photograph.

But it didn't make sense! The photograph was understandable. It was to hold Ben to his disguise and his job. But why should he draw the police's attention to No. 19 Billiter Road, which would surely be as embarrassing to him as to his new caretaker? And then no one could have seen Ben entering this house of his own free will! He had been carried in, unconscious . . .

'Come, come!' The constable's voice broke in on Ben's cogitations, and now there was a new note in it. 'Let's get on! I haven't got all night to waste! Maybe after all this fellow we're after won't prove as black as he sounds— maybe he'll be able to clear himself altogether, once we contact him.' His large eyes fixed themselves on Ben's as he bent forward on his stair. 'If you want the truth, I'm not too sure of our informant, and that's a fact! Because, look! What did he want to take that photograph for? It might have been some sort of a plant to fix the blame on the wrong person! And why did he hang around after taking it? Why didn't he move off at once?' The policeman rose, and moving forward tapped Ben on the shoulder. '*And what's going on in this house?* Something fishy, I'll be bound! Come out with all you know, and you'll be on safe ground. Hold anything back, and before we've finished you may be for it! This is the moment to snap out of any tangle you may be in, and you mayn't get another! So which is it to be? Have you got anything to tell me—or have you?'

Ben took a deep breath. Here was his chance being handed to him on a platter! But he did not take it.

'No, I ain't got nothink ter tell yer,' he answered, shortly.

The constable frowned.

'You wouldn't care to change your mind about that, sonny?' he asked.

71

'I'll mike up somethink if yer like,' retorted Ben.

'I'm afraid that wouldn't help.'

'Then I can't give yer none. This is a respeckerble 'ouse, no one like that there pickcher's bin 'ere, and I wanter git back ter bed.'

'I see. You're not talking?'

'There's nothink ter tork abart.'

'Your employer might find something if I called on him.'

'I ain't stoppin' yer.'

'What is his name? You haven't told me?'

'I 'aven't bin engaiged ter give hinfermashun.'

'Does that also apply to his address?'

'If yer wanter write to 'im, jest pop it through the letter-box and I'll see 'e gits it.'

The policeman nodded. Then he straightened himself, and moved towards the front door.

'Very well, then,' he said. 'For the moment we'll leave it at that. But I'll be seeing you again in the morning.' He opened the door. 'And that's a promise!'

Ben gazed at the door for several seconds after it had closed. Then he leapt into the air as something soft touched his leg. But it was only Sammy.

10

Conference on the Stairs

'I owe yer one fer that, Sammy,' said Ben, reproachfully. 'Yer orter sahnd yer 'ooter afore yer comes! See, me nerves ain't wot they was, and wot they was wer'n' never nothink ter shaht abart. But yer the on'y friend I got in this 'ere blinkin' 'ouse, so we carn't afford ter quarrel, can we? Let's sit dahn and 'ave a jaw, 'cos I want ter know wot yer think abart that bobby.'

He sat down on the stair lately occupied by the policeman, and the cat leapt upon his lap, as though to show there was no ill feeling. Funny about cats. Some you fair hated. Take them white 'uns—Simonese, wasn't they called? See 'em in a garden when it's getting dark and they looked like ghosts. But some was nice. This 'un was.

'Now, I dessay yer wondered, if yer was anywhere abart while I was torkin' to 'im,' went on Ben, 'why I didn't come aht with the trooth, and it's a fack there was more'n one time when I was goin' ter charnce it. Fust I was, and then I wasn't, and then I wasn't, and then I was. If yer git me? And when, jest afore 'e goes, and sayin' 'e'd be back in the mornin', 'e gives me a 'int that it might be orl right fer me if I spilled aht the lot and that 'e was ready ter put the blime on Smith instead o' me—well, there was a charnce, if yer like? Corse, bobbies are up ter orl the tricks, and 'e might of sed that jest ter mike me feel sife and tork. Is that the way you sized it up, Sammy?'

Sammy refused to commit itself.

'Well, it might o' bin that, but it wer'n't the way *I* sized it up. See, wot I thort was this. 'Ow did 'e know so much abart Smith? Do yer remember 'im sayin', "Why did 'e 'ang rahnd arter taikin' the photergraph, why didn't 'e move orf at once?" Smith must of bin a fool ter tell 'im that! But 'e must of bin a bigger fool ter give a bobby this address, and even if 'e did, why should the bobby think somethink was goin' on 'ere? Do yer git wot I'm drivin' at, eh?'

Again Sammy gave no indication of its thoughts, but went on purring.

'And then,' continued Ben, fixing his eyes on the flickering candle on the floor, 'if we tike it a bit further back, 'ere's the pleece comin' along abart a murder, with a photo of the bloke they're lookin' for—that's me—but orl they sends is jest one constable. If I'd bin 'ere, wich I was, I might 'ave 'ad a gun, so wouldn't yer think there'd be a cupple, and one of 'em 'ud be a sergeant, if no 'igher?'

Sammy stopped purring for a moment. Impressed at last? When the purring was resumed, it had increased in volume.

'Ah, I see yer thinks like I does,' said Ben. 'Yer thinks it's fishy! Yer thinks that the way 'e acted and some o' the things 'e sed wasn't exackly wot yer'd expeck from the pleece. In fact, Sammy, yer think 'e wasn't no constable at all, but jest playin' at it! Yer do? Well, we're a pair, 'cos so do I!'

The candle spluttered and nearly went out. He stretched forward and slid it out of the draught that was coming through the crack under the front door.

'All right! Nah where do we git? If 'e wasn't no constable, wot did 'ooever 'e was want ter go pertendin' for? Well, that'd depend on 'oo 'e was, wouldn't it, and 'e wasn't Smith, that I'll lay. I'd 'ave twigged Smith fust go. But s'pose 'e was Smith's pal wot 'elped ter bring me along 'ere? Then corse 'e'd know the answers to orl the questions 'e arsked, and 'e'd on'y arsk 'em ter see if I'd give the show away, or if I could be trusted like. "Are yer sure of this bloke?" p'r'aps Smith's pal sez, meanin' me. "I put the fear o' Gawd on 'im," sez Smith, wich is right, 'cos 'e did! "But wot if you've mide 'im more afeard o' you than of the pleece?" sez Smith's pal. "Ah, I git yer," sez Smith, "yer mean 'e might spill the beans if 'e got the charnce, but 'ow's 'e goin' ter git the charnce?" "'E'd 'ave one if a bobby called," sez Smith's pal. "Well, we'll 'ave one call," sez Smith, "and see if 'e tikes the charnce? If 'e doesn't we'll know 'e's okay, but if 'e does and spills the beans, we'll finish 'im."'

He paused, surprised and gratified by his own cleverness, and then completed his reconstruction.

'So then, Sammy, they decide that the pal's the one ter come, 'cos 'e's the one I wouldn't reckernise, see, but don't arsk me 'ow they got the bobby's clothes and 'elmet, I'll let that one go. Any'ow, along 'e comes, and if I'd fallen fer it I'd of bin Corpse Nummer Three! But I keeps me 'ead, and I don't let on nothink, and now orf 'e's gone agine ter tell Smith wot a good boy I am! "'Ow did it go?" sez Smith. "It went a fair treat," sez 'is pal. "'E didn't give us away?" sez Smith. "Not a heyelash," sez 'is pal, "and I fooled 'im proper." "Then 'e's the bloke we want," sez Smith, "and termorrer we can git on with it."'

Ben paused again, this time not so happily. 'Git on with wot?' he muttered.

Well, that was what he was staying on at Number Nineteen to find out, wasn't it? Course it was. To find out. But his tired brain, rebelling against overwork, now refused to help him any more, and his tired eyes blinked enviously at the sleeping cat on his lap. What about a bit of sleep himself? Time you and me moved, Sammy, ain't it? He closed his eyes for a moment. When he opened them, he rubbed them.

The candle was out, and the first hint of dawn was creeping greyly through the hall, and he was still on the stairs.

'Go on!' he said. 'Am I 'ere?'

11

Discoveries in the Dawn

Well, after all, it was not so surprising, for Ben had slept in plenty of other unusual places. Once he had slept up a chimney, to the mutual discomfort of himself and the maid who had come down in the morning to light the fire. Compared with that, a staircase was a palace.

He did not move for a little while. He had to play a little game with himself first. It was by no means the first time he had played it. You won if you could wrap the solid realities of the night before into the filmy substance of a dream. Of course, you never won it, and Ben did not make history now by winning it. The corpses wouldn't stay in the parcel. And after all, even if they had, what would he be doing here, sitting on a stair with a cat in his lap?

No, not the cat. That had dissolved, anyway. He looked around for it vaguely.

'I s'pose yer 'as ter 'ave a walk sometimes,' he reflected, 'but I wish yer wasn't so fond o' the vanishin' act!'

He felt a bit lost and lonely without it. The day that

was beginning to percolate around him wasn't going to be nice, it wasn't going to be at all nice, and you wanted someone to talk to. How about looking for it?

He called. 'Oi, Sammy! Where've yer got ter?' The sound of his voice was unsatisfactory. Different, somehow. Something gone wrong with his swallow? It did sometimes first thing in the morning. See, you don't swallow in your sleep, so it needs sort of oiling. But another reason might be that things sound different in different lights. A cough in the sunshine isn't the same as a cough by a flickering candle, and the acoustics of dawn have a special quality of their own, though Ben could not have put it in those words.

But when the cat did not respond with its reappearance, it was not merely dislike of his own early morning voice that prevented him from calling it again. He had been asleep for a number of hours, and this meant that he had lost touch with the immediate sequence of events. A lot can happen while you are asleep. In a house like this it was a gift if you ever woke up again! Ben had woken up again, however, and his priority job was to go over the place to see whether everything was just as he had left it. He wanted to be sure there were no more corpses lying around.

He went upstairs first, keeping an eye skinned for the cat as he went. He didn't want it to come slithering through his legs while he wasn't watching. He found no change on the first floor, apart from its changed appearance in the gradually growing daylight. There was one little thing that vaguely troubled him, though. A drip-drip-drip from the bathroom turned out to be the cold tap over the bath. That was better than the blood he had at first imagined it might be, but he thought he had turned the tap off after putting his head under it. He made a special point of turning taps off, because the sound of dripping was nobody's nerve cure. Well, he supposed that this time he had been a bit careless, concentrating his attention instead on his dripping head.

The second floor gave him another small worry. Nothing looked different bar the door. 'Didn't I leave it open?' he asked himself. The last time he had left the room was when he had woken up and chased the unknown Thing that had awakened him. He cast his mind back to that unpleasant occasion, trying to recall details. 'I gits orf the bed, and I goes ter the door, and I runs aht. No, 'arf a mo'! Afore I runs aht I remembers the candle, yus, that's right, so I stops and I turns, and I goes ter the manting-piece.' He looked towards the mantelpiece. Okay. One candlestick still there, t'other gone. 'I lights the candle, and I goes back ter the door—I goes back ter the door—yus, I goes back ter the door—and when I'm ahtside—?'

In vain he tried to visualise himself closing the door behind him. The picture would not come. Of course, you often did things and forgot you had afterwards. Take a kitchen clock. You wind it and put it back, and as like as not you say a couple of minutes later, 'Oh, I must wind the kitchen clock,' and find you've wound it. So he might have closed the door. Only why *would* he close it? He was in a hurry, wasn't he? When you're in a hurry, you don't waste time closing doors.

Trying not to feel depressed, and still having found no sign of his feline companion, he went down again, inves-tigated the ground floor, and then, taking a deep breath, descended to the basement. And in the kitchen he found something which, without any doubt whatever, was not as he had left it. The kitchen table had been without anything upon it, barring a soiled tablecloth, when he had last been in the room. Now the table bore a pint bottle of milk and a sandwich loaf!

'Some 'un *as* bin 'ere!' muttered Ben. 'Bin 'ere while I slep'! Lummy!'

Who? The question was answered a moment later when he moved the milk bottle to reveal a sheet of paper under it. On the sheet was scribbled the following note:

'Dear Mr Jones Je Ne Pense Pas,

'If you are awake when I pay my next call, and you may not be as I intend to call very early and you are sleeping most soundly at this moment (why have you chosen the stairs, by the way—isn't the bed comfortable?) I shall be interested to learn how you have been getting on. So far you seem to have been quite a good boy, but before I can be perfectly, perfectly certain of you and trust you with fuller responsibility I shall require a complete account of all that has happened since our last happy meeting, whether there have been any incidents or discoveries that need discussing, and whether there have been any callers. You will find me particularly interested in the callers, so be sure you do not leave any out. That, I assure you, Mr Jones, would be very, very foolish indeed. The fact that I have called myself without your knowing anything about it until you read these words will prove to you that you are not immune from observation, and that you may be watched at times when you least suspect it. Can you even say for certain that you are not being watched at the very moment you are reading these lines? Life is very uncertain, Mr Jones, as someone found yesterday on a park seat, you may remember, and it is so easy to make a fatal slip, is it not? But life also has its compensations, two of which you will find on this table. I do not want you to go out and do any shopping this morning, so the milk and bread will save you the trouble. Also, you might meet a paper-man who is selling your picture to the British Public. Outside this house you will be famous today, Mr Jones. That is why you will be so wise to stay in it.

'Yours till our next,

'Mr Smith, also Je Ne Pense Pas.'

Ben read the letter through slowly, and then read it through again more slowly. It was all pretty clear barring Je Ne Pense Pas and Immune. 'I expeck they're somethink rude,' he decided. Anyway, the important thing was that Mr Smith had been here—corse, 'e'd 'ave a latchkey—and that he was coming again. Meanwhile, food was necessary to stoke up for the troubles to come.

As he was about to start his breakfast preparations it occurred to him that he had not quite completed his search, and that the dark passage containing the locked door was still to be investigated. Should he go there now, and get it over? On the other hand, why go there at all? He knew what lay on the other side of the locked door, and could not see what was to be gained by a second penny peep. Moreover, the Thing had come down the basement stairs, and if it was still anywhere about, up that dark passage it was most likely to be! Surely that was a most excellent reason for staying where one was?

So Ben stayed, voyaging no farther than the larder, which was reached through a door from the kitchen. In the larder he found Mr Smith.

'Gawd!' he gasped.

'You could not have put it better,' answered Mr Smith. 'How are you?'

For a moment, indignation overcame all other emotions.

'Wotcher want ter go playin' tricks like this for?' exclaimed Ben.

'Being in the larder is not a trick,' replied Mr Smith.

'Well, never mind wot yer calls it, I won't be no use to yer if yer give me 'eart disease! If yer was 'ere why did yer write me a note like yer wasn't?'

'The note warned you. Didn't it say perhaps you were being watched while you read it? Well, you were. Every moment. I had an excellent view. You scratched yourself five times and rubbed your nose twice. Now let me watch you have your breakfast, and we can talk while you eat.'

'No, thanks,' retorted Ben. 'When I torks I torks, and when I eats I eats, I don't berlieve in mixin' 'em. So we'll tork fust, if it's orl the sime ter you!'

His indignation had given him a brave start, and he decided to keep up the bravery as long as he could. Once you let the other fellow get on top of you, you're sunk.

'I've no objection,' Mr Smith responded, now moving out of the larder and sitting down on a kitchen chair. 'I haven't really come to see a show, and you know what you've got to talk about.'

'There's one thing I'd like ter tork abart,' said Ben. ''Ow did yer git in?'

'You don't really suppose I have to ring, do you?'

'Oh. Yer got a latch-key?'

'Obviously.'

'I see. But s'pose I'd bolted the door?'

'Why suppose it, since you didn't?'

'If I did next time, yer'd have ter ring?'

'I doubt it.'

'Oh! Yer mean—?'

'Never mind what I mean,' Mr Smith interrupted sharply. 'Don't waste more time, but give me your report!'

'Oh! It's a report wot I'm givin', is it? Okay. 'Ere's one. Some'un come in the 'ouse in the night, and 'e went up inter the bathroom and left the tap drippin'.'

'Probably myself. Next?'

'Eh?'

'Have you had any callers while you were awake?'

'I 'ad one.'

'Who?'

Now they were coming to it. Ben kept his mind steady.

'Yus, and yer won't like ter 'ear this!'

'You alarm me?'

'If yer want the truth—'

'I want nothing else.'

'Orl right, yer gittin' it! It alarmed me, too. See, it was a bobby!'

Ben stared at Mr Smith with what he hoped was the proper expression of apprehension. He felt he was not doing too badly, and he prayed he could keep it up. Meanwhile, Mr Smith gazed back, his own expression giving nothing away.

'Really? A bobby?' repeated Mr Smith.

'Yus. And 'e come abart the—you know what!'

Mr Smith nodded thoughtfully. 'And what did he ask you?' he enquired.

''E wanted ter know if I knoo anythink abart me,' answered Ben, 'if yer git me, and 'e showed me that photo you took! Yus, and I ain't thankin' yer fer that!'

'I wouldn't expect you to,' responded Mr Smith. 'Yes? Go on.'

But Ben was discovering that it was by no means easy to go on, the situation being perplexingly subtle for his simple mind. The situation was that he had to pretend he had believed the policeman genuine, and he had to tell his story to one who already knew all its details. Nor was this all. He had to pretend further that he did not know Mr Smith knew them, and if by any slip he gave himself away it would be revealed that he had recognised the fake, and he would lose the credit he was trying to establish for having sent the constable off empty-handed.

'Go on,' repeated Mr Smith.

'I'm goin' on,' said Ben, 'but afore I do, you might tell me why yer showed 'em that pickcher!'

'But you already know that. To keep you indoors.'

'Meanin' yer didn't want me ter 'ave the charnce of splittin' to a bobby?'

'In spite of its rashness, you might have done so in a moment of lunacy.'

'Oh! Well, did I 'ave a moment o' loonercy larst night when I didn't 'ave ter go ter no bobby 'cos 'e come ter me?'

'You're going to tell *me* that.'

'Orl right. Then I didn't. 'E arsked a lot o' questions,

but 'e didn't git no chinge out o' me. P'r'aps if 'e 'ad, 'e'd of bin 'ere waitin' fer yer when yer come.'

That, Ben thought, was rather good.

'Go on,' said Mr Smith.

Blast him! How much longer was he supposed to go on? Why wouldn't Mr Smith own up and end the silly game? The test had served its purpose—at least, Mr Smith would think it had—so what was the object of making Ben repeat what was already known?

'I carn't give the 'ole conversashun.'

'I'm not asking you to. If you discussed the weather you can leave that out. What brought him?'

'Eh?'

'What made him come to this house?'

'Well, yer give 'im the photo, didn't yer?'

'There was no address on it.'

'Corse there wasn't. You must of give it to 'im along with the photo, and if that wasn't daft—'

Whoa! He was getting into dangerous water! It was the daftness of this that had weakened the genuine aspect of the whole episode, for it was quite obvious that Mr Smith would never have given the address away. Yes, but half a mo'! The policeman hadn't said anything about that. That was what Ben had thought—wasn't it?—when the policeman had said the other thing? What was the other thing? Keep yer mind steady! What was it? The trouble was that Mr Smith was looking at him hard, and you can't think so easy when people look at you hard. Why didn't he own up? Lummy! Was the reason that he hadn't anything to own up to? Was Ben wrong, and had it been a real bobby, after all!

'You seem in trouble,' said Mr Smith.

'It's on'y that I jest thort o' somethink,' answered Ben.

'What?'

'That's right—on'y jest remembered it.'

'Let's have it then.'

Fortunately, at that moment, Ben did remember it.

'Well, see, it was like this. Corse, you didn't give 'im the address. Yer ain't sich a mug as that!'

'Thank you.'

'Wot the bobby sed, and wot I'd fergot, was that 'e'd come 'cos some'un 'ad seed me come in 'ere.'

'I see.'

'Do yer? Well, I don't!'

'What don't you see?'

'Well, I was brort 'ere subconshus, wasn't I.'

'That's one way to put it.'

'And it was you wot brort me, wasn't it?'

'I did perform you that service.'

'Yus, one day, when I get a 'ole week, I'm goin' ter write and thank yer. But if yer was doin' me a service, like yer sed, I don't s'pose yer carried me in 'ere not with nobody watchin', and even if they was watchin', 'ow'd they recker-nise me? I was okay in the pickcher, but yer looks dif'rent when yer subconshus.'

Mr Smith appeared amused. Ben couldn't see what was funny.

'You certainly looked different when you came out of your subconsciousness,' he remarked, 'but let us leave that point. You have nothing more to tell me about this policeman?'

'Yus, I 'ave,' replied Ben, suddenly realising how he could finally prove whether the policeman had been the real thing or not—or, at any rate, whether Mr Smith believed him so. 'I've got ter warn yer!'

'Really?'

'Yus! 'E's callin' agine. In the mornin', 'e sed. 'Is larst words was, "That's a promise!" So we gotter look aht—ain't we?'

Now Ben watched Mr Smith as closely as Mr Smith was watching him. Mr Smith showed no sign of alarm. On the contrary, he smiled again.

'Don't worry about that bobby, Mr Jones,' he said. 'He won't call again. I happen to know that you were not the last person to see him last night. Somebody else saw him, and he has been dealt with.'

'Dealt with?'

'Dealt with. Such a useful term, don't you think? So let us forget him, and now tell me if he was your only visitor? And remember,' he added, 'I may already know a little more than you think.'

Now Ben found himself facing a fresh problem. There had been another visitor, but this was one he did not want to talk about. He recognised Mr Smith's warning, however, and he recalled the sudden departure of the visitor, and also the footsteps he had heard along the street just after she vanished. He had believed them at the time to be those of the man now so shrewdly watching him. He knew that Mr Smith had spent quite a lot of time watching. Suppose he *had* seen the lady go? And suppose, having seen her, he heard Ben declare that she had not been? That would upset the apple-cart proper . . .

'What I like about you, Mr Jones,' said Mr Smith, 'is that you answer all my questions so quickly. Lightning isn't in it.'

'I won't say wot I like abart you,' retorted Ben, ''cos I carn't find it.'

'Did you have any other visitor?'

'Eh?'

'You haven't seen me really angry yet, have you?'

'I've seed yer lots of hother things.'

'But not angry. You'd be surprised.'

He spoke truly, for the hand that suddenly thumped on the table made both Ben and the milk bottle jump.

'HAVE YOU?'

'Well, as a matter o' fack—'

'As a matter of fact,' said Mr Smith, now quiet again, 'you have?'

'Yus.'

'Thank you. Man, woman, or child?'

'Well, it was a woman.'

'Go on.'

'I'm goin' on, but yer keeps on stoppin' me goin' on tellin' me ter!' Ben's voice was indignant. He had not quite got over that thump. Lummy, wot did they think yer was mide of? Iron? 'It was a woman, and she rings the bell, and dahn I goes and opens the door. See, I was up at the top, so that's why I 'ad ter go dahn.'

'Spare me unnecessary details!'

'Oh! Well, some likes 'em. I come dahn, like I sed, and I opens the door, and there's this lidy, standin' there. I didn't like it. That's a fack. No I didn't.'

'What did she want?'

'Well, there yer are!'

'I'm afraid I am not.'

'Wot I mean is, yer'll never guess. Wot I mean is— well, it was a wash-aht. Yus, and arter bringin' me dahn orl them stairs. See, I was jest gettin' comfertible with Sammy—'

'I beg your pardon?'

'Eh?'

'Who may Sammy be?'

'Oh!' Blast his tongue! But, come to think of it, was there any reason for keeping Sammy dark? Lummy, you didn't know what was safe to say and what wasn't, but Sammy ought to be okay, and while he was talking about Sammy he could be thinking about the woman. 'Corse, yer doesn't know abart Sammy.'

'Is this another caller?'

'Well, in a way, it was.'

'Someone who called before the woman?'

'That's right. Sammy, the woman, the bobby. That's ow they come. But, corse, Sammy wer'n't nothink ter worry abart. It was jest a cat wot walked in, and it come upstairs with me like. Come ter that, yer must of seed 'im, 'cos 'e was on me lap on the stairs. Leastwise, 'e was when I went orf, but not when I woke up.'

An impatient movement from Mr Smith, and an ominous expression, warned Ben that Sammy had had his day. Fortunately, he had also had his use, for while rambling on about the cat Ben had thought of a solution about the woman.

'Yus, but wot yer wanter 'ear abart is the lidy,' he said, quickly, 'and wot she come for. 'Is Mr Bloomersbury in?' she asks. "'Oo's Mr Bloomersbury?" I sez. "Don't 'e live 'ere?" she sez. "No, 'e don't," I sez, and then it comes aht that she'd come ter the wrong address. Yus, that was it, arter bringin' me dahn orl them stairs! Would yer believe it?'

The question was less whether Mr Smith *would* believe it than whether he did.

'Do you mean she had been given the wrong address?' asked Mr Smith.

'No, come ter it,' replied Ben.

'Then she knew the address she wanted?'

'Eh?'

'Then she—'

'Yus, I 'eard yer—yus!'

'Yes she knew the address, or yes you heard me?'

'Both.'

'What address did she mean to go to?'

'I didn't ask her.'

'Why not?'

'Why would I? I didn't wanter go and see no Mr Bloomersbury!'

'I should have thought she would have mentioned the address?'

'Well, there yer are. One thinks a lot o' things wot ain't. Once I thort I'd never go in fer side-whiskies. But if yer wants it,' went on Ben, gathering that Mr Smith did, 'she'd got the number right, but she thort she was in another street. "Wot street's this?" she sez. "Billiter," I sez. "I must of took the wrong turnin'," she sez. Is that enough abart it, or do yer want some more?'

'How did she leave?'

'On 'er feet.'

'That's not funny.'

'I know it ain't, but I don't git yer.'

'Did she just apologise and go, or—did her mistake seem to worry her in any way?'

Then Ben did get him. Mr Smith *had* seen her depart!

'Oh, that! Well, yus, she did seem a bit upset like. You know—bringin' me dahn orl them stairs for nothink. I expeck I was a bit cross, and I ain't no more nice not when I'm cross than you are. Yus, nah I comes ter think of it, orl at once she gits in a proper flurry, and runs dahn the front steps and vanishes afore yer could say Jack Robinson!'

Mr Smith took out a pencil and tapped the lead end on the table. Then his fingers twisted it round and he tapped with the other end. Then he reversed it again, repeating the process half-a-dozen times. His expression, meanwhile, was thoughtful.

'Yer must teach me that,' said Ben.

'You may be taught a lot of things before you are many hours older,' replied Mr Smith, 'but we'll leave this till later.'

'Wot else are yer goin' ter teach me?'

'You'll find out. Fortunately, you seem quite a good learner. And now have you told me everything?'

Ben hesitated.

'I see you haven't.'

'Well—that's orl the callers.'

'Let's have the rest?'

'Well, I thort I 'eard some'un abart the 'ouse in the night.'

'Oh? You did?'

'Yus.'

'What did you do?'

'Got aht o' bed.'

'Where did the sounds come from?'

'They was in the passidge when I got aht o' bed, but afore that they was goin' along beside the river.'

'River?'

'That's right. See, I was floatin' in it.'

'Mr Jones,' said Mr Smith, 'are you right in the head?'

'If I ain't, it's my 'ead, so why worry? But wot abart your 'ead? If yer was ter tell me that in the middle o' the night yer was flying in the sky with a cupple o' saucers in yer 'ands, would I 'ave ter arsk yer if yer was dreamin'? *I* was floatin' on the river when this shuffle come along the tow-path, but when I woke up it was aht in the passidge, like I sed, so I 'ops aht o' bed, like I sed, and went dahn arter it, and I was jest ketchin' it up at the top o' the bisement stairs when the front door went and the copper come.'

'I think I see.'

'Well, yer better mike sure.'

'And what did you do after the copper had gone?'

'I sat on the stairs ter 'ave a think, and when I opened me eyes it was mornin'.'

'And then?'

'Yer don't want nothink, do yer? Yer better give me a diary so's I can put dahn the times I sneezes! Then I went over the 'ouse ter see if there was any more corpses, but I didn't find none.'

'More corpses?' murmured Mr Smith.

'Eh?'

'Wasn't that what you said?'

'Yus.'

'Meaning you had found some others?'

That was precisely what Ben had meant, but he was not sure whether he had meant to mention it.

'Yer ain't fergot the one on the seat?' he replied, cautiously.

'That one was in a park. Have you found any inside this house?'

'Where'd I find 'em? I don't s'pose, if you'd left any be'ind, yer'd leave 'em lyin' abart like chairs and taibles!'

'True enough—but in that case why look for them?'

'That's one ter you,' admitted Ben, and then suddenly took the plunge. 'There's on'y one plice where they'd be—sayin' there was any.'

'Where is that?'

'Do I 'ave ter tell yer?'

'I have asked you to.'

'Orl right. 'Ow abart be'ind the locked door along the passidge?'

Mr Smith raised his eyebrows. He did not answer for a few seconds, filling the time by playing his little game with his pencil. Then he got up from his chair.

'You know, that's quite an idea, Mr Jones,' he said. 'Quite an idea. Let's go and have a look!'

'Eh?'

'Come along!'

'Yer mean—yer've got a key?'

'Could we look,' replied Mr Smith, 'if I hadn't?'

He moved to the door. Ben hesitated, then reluctantly followed him.

It was a short but unpleasant journey from the kitchen to the passage with the locked door, and while they made it Ben wondered whether he was about to get a closer view of a sight which would spoil his appetite for breakfast. When the door was reached he stood behind Mr Smith while he inserted a key he had produced from his pocket. The key turned noiselessly, and the door, in response to a push, swung slowly inwards into dim space. There was a damp and musty smell that made Ben think of tombs.

'Well?' said Mr Smith.

Ben gazed round a large empty cellar. Such light as there was came from a grating high up on one of the walls, by which were faintly discerned two things that broke the bareness of the gloomy space. One was, presumably, a low cupboard door. The other was something lying dead on the floor. But it was not a human corpse. It was Sammy, the cat.

12

Ben Receives Instructions

'Well?' repeated Mr Smith.

Again Ben did not reply. He was trying to get out of a red mist that had suddenly filled the cellar at the sight of the dead cat.

Ben never liked seeing dead things, but he had seen so many human corpses in his troubled life that, in a sense, he had got used to them. That did not mean, of course, that they could not make him run; just that as a rule he thought more about himself than the corpses at their meetings. But he could never get used to seeing dead animals. See, they 'adn't 'ad no charnce. One of the reasons he enjoyed cheese, quite apart from the wonderful taste of it, was that you didn't have to kill anything to get it. You just did something to milk, which couldn't feel, and lo! there was cheese! It wasn't like that with animals. They, well, sort of trusted you, especially when they were the kind you made companions of. Sammy had been Ben's companion. He'd taken to it, and they'd slept together—and now, here it was lying dead, with its head looking as if someone had . . .

'It is only a cat,' said Mr Smith.

He was looking at Ben curiously.

'That's right,' muttered Ben.

'The one, I take it, you referred to?'

'That's right. 'Oo done it?'

'I did not,' Mr Smith replied, 'if that is what you are thinking. People like you and I, Mr Jones, would hardly waste our efforts on such small fry. Please interpret your emotions for me. Is it grief for a departed feline—or just surprise?'

There was something in Mr Smith's tone, and also in his expression, that warned Ben against revealing the truth of his feelings. He was trying to build himself up as a hard-boiled crook, or at any rate as a man who was prepared to participate in criminal crookedness, and acute sorrow over the demise of a cat was not consistent with the role. He decided therefore that it would be safer to plump for the surprise, and he gathered from Mr Smith's reception of the false information that he had chosen wisely.

'I am relieved,' said Mr Smith, 'for you are going to have far more than the death of a cat to face before you have finished. But why the surprise? Or, rather, so much of it? Did you expect to see something else?'

'Wot else?' replied Ben, cautiously.

'True—what else could you expect, since you were not really in a position to expect anything? Or were you?'

''Ow could I be?'

'That was my point. You could only have expected to find something here if you had already been in the room.'

'That's right.'

'And you haven't been in the room.'

'That's right.'

'Or have you?'

'Now I comes ter think of it, corse I 'ave. As I 'adn't got no key I jest took the door orf the 'inges! Fancy me fergettin'!' Feigning indignation, he went on, ''Ow many more times 'ave I got ter tell yer? Yer mikin' so much of it, seems like there was somethink 'ere I wasn't s'posed ter see—so now wot abart *me* arskin' a bit? Was there?'

Mr Smith rubbed his chin, and then smiled.

'As a matter of fact, Mr Jones, there was,' he said.

'Oh, there was?'

'There was.'

'Wot?'

'Yes, I think I'll tell you.'

'Well, 'ow abart doin' it?'

'Our last caretaker was in this room,' said Mr Smith.

'Oh!' muttered Ben. 'So *that's* 'oo 'e was!'

'Who what was?'

'Eh? Well, the chap yer tellin' me abart, ain't it?'

'You did know, then, that there was a chap?'

'You've just said so!'

'And you have just confirmed my impression that you already knew it, though you may not have been certain of the chap's identity. What was he doing? Knitting?'

''Ere,' complained Ben. 'I've 'ad enough o' this.'

'But I haven't, quite,' replied Mr Smith. 'You see, I am wondering how—' He turned and glanced towards the door. Suddenly he cracked his fingers. 'But of course! How simple! The keyhole!'

He turned back to Ben, his eyebrows raised enquiringly. Feeling he was losing whatever advantage he may have had, Ben tried to regain it.

'Well, s'pose I did 'ave a peep through the key'ole?' he

retorted, 'wot was there against that? If you was alone with a locked door, wouldn't you try a squint?'

'I very likely would,' answered Mr Smith, 'but I would not keep anything I saw from those I was supposed to be working with.'

'You've kep' plenty from me, and that's wot I wanter know! *Am* I workin' with you? If I am, why doncher put me wise proper?'

Ignoring the question, Mr Smith again turned to the door, and then took Ben's arm. 'Come outside for a moment,' he said, and led him out into the passage.

'Wot's this abart?' demanded Ben.

'You'll see in a moment,' replied Mr Smith.

He closed the door, and then put his eye to the keyhole. Then he stood away, and ordered Ben to do it. While Ben's eye peered through, Mr Smith enquired behind him,

'What do you see now?'

'Nothink,' answered Ben.

'Nothing at all?'

'Ain't I sed so?'

'What time did you look through the keyhole last night?'

'Why?'

'What time—'

''Ow do I know? I ain't got no watch, and even if I 'ad why would I write it dahn? At two minits past seven I coughed, at three past I scratched a tickle, at four past I looked through a key'ole. Some of the questions yer arsk'd mike a kipper cry!'

'Whatever time it was, I expect it was dark?'

'Yus. Yer can 'ave that one.'

'Darker than it is now.'

'Eh?'

'I have not known you for twenty-four hours, yet in that time I must have heard you say "Eh" over a thousand times. Would you try and vary it a little? It must have been darker, for now a little light is coming into the cellar through the grating. Yet you can still see nothing. How, then, did you see anything yesterday when you were looking through the keyhole?'

'I 'aven't sed—'

'No, but I'm saying it. Be very careful, Mr Jones. You're either going to make a lot of money or you're going to lie on the floor just as you saw the last caretaker doing—and as the cat is now doing. It's up to you. You may as well admit what I already know, and what you should have told me at once. You saw the caretaker lying dead, didn't you?'

Ben gave up.

'Orl right, orl right,' he grunted. 'I did. And I didn't tell yer 'cos I thort it'd be better if you told me, knowin' yer must of knowed it. And if yer don't git that, I carn't 'elp yer!'

'What I don't get is how you saw the corpse, and that's what you're going to tell me. One more lie, and you're finished.' Something pressed into Ben's back. Mr Smith, still behind him, laughed. 'Only my finger, Mr Jones. But next time it won't be. Answer my question. One—two—'

'Some'un switched on a torch.'

'Ah! And then?'

'That's orl. I'd seed enough!'

'What you saw being the corpse and the person with the torch?'

'I didn't want ter see no more.'

'Did you see enough to describe to me the person with the torch?'

'No, I didn't.'

'Try. Have a shot.'

'I tell yer, I didn't. When some'un's standin' in the darkness with a torch, orl yer sees is wot the torch is on. It was on the corpse. I saw '*im*!'

'Rather a thin man?'

'Well, most of 'em looks thin when they're dead. Sort of like they'd bin punchered. But the one with the torch, 'e was orl in the shadder.'

'Nevertheless,' suggested Mr Smith, 'I expect you saw enough to know it wasn't a giraffe or an elephant?'

'Eh? Oh! Well, corse! Wotcher gittin' at?'

'Or whether it was a man or a woman?'

'It was a man.'

'So you did see him a bit, then. Was he tall? Short? Bald? Hairy? Did you see his feet?'

Feet? What did he want to know that for? And why did the question vaguely worry Ben? Feet—something about feet. What was it?

'I carn't tell yer nothink not more'n I've told yer,' replied Ben, 'so it's no use goin' on arskin'. But wot *I* wanter know is where did 'e come from, and where did 'e go ter, seein' 'e ain't there now, no more than the corpse is! I can see *you* know 'oo 'e is, so ain't it time yer told me? Wot do I do if 'e comes poppin' aht arter me when you've gorn?' Feet . . . Feet . . . 'Yus, and wotcher want ter know abart 'is feet for? Is anythink wrong with 'em? . . . Lummy, does they sahnd like a wet sponge when yer 'ears 'em?'

Mr Smith did not answer. He seemed to be thinking

rather hard. So was Ben. He was thinking of the crunching sound of the footsteps he had heard in the night.

'Nah, listen!' he said, earnestly. 'I can stand a lot, well, ain't I done it, and play fair with me and I'll do the job I'm 'ere for, but there's one thing I bar. I ain't goin' ter be left 'ere alone with no monnertrocity! I see a cubberd in the cellar. I wancher to open it, jest ter show me it ain't there. See, yer sed yer'd got a gun, so if it is there and mikes trouble yer'll be able ter deal with it when I couldn't. That mikes sense, don't it?'

Mr Smith shook his head.

'The most sensible thing to do,' he answered, 'will be to let sleeping dogs lie for the moment—or perhaps I should say cats—and get back to the kitchen to finish our conversation there.' He moved to the cellar door as he spoke and relocked it. 'There's not much more. And then you can have your breakfast.'

'Yus, and wot do I do if the monnertrocity comes in while I'm 'avin' it ter join me?' replied Ben.

'He won't. Don't argue. I've got to get back to my own breakfast. Come along!'

Back in the kitchen, Mr Smith took a small sealed packet from his pocket, and handed it to Ben.

'This morning, at half-past ten,' he said, 'someone will call to look over the house. The house-agent will be with him. If the agent asks you whether you have anything for him, give him that packet, and then be ready to assist him in any way he may require. And when I say any way, I mean any way. Do you get that?'

Ben nodded.

'He may not require your help. In that case you will go up to the top room and wait until he comes for you, or until he goes. After he has gone, just carry on here as usual until you get your next orders. Now is all that clear?'

'Clear as ditchwater,' answered Ben.

'Just to make sure, repeat what you've got to do.'

'At 'arf-past ten the bell's goin' ter ring and I'm goin' ter let in a 'ouse-'unter and a 'ouse-agent. I'm ter give the 'ouse-agent this 'ere packet wot 'e arsks for, and if 'e arsks me ter 'elp 'im from lendin' 'im me pocket-'ankerchiff ter 'ittin' the 'ouse-'unter on the 'ead, I'm ter 'elp 'im, but if 'e don't want no 'elp then I'm ter go up and sit on me thumbs till the clouds roll by.'

'Admirable!' exclaimed Mr Smith. 'I think you'll do! To be quite frank with you I have had my moments of doubt, but I believe that you know by now which side your bread is buttered—'

'And I'm waitin' fer the jam!'

'You shall have it, if you behave.'

'I be'aved orl right, didn't I,' Ben reminded him, 'when that bobby called larst night?'

'Keep on like that, and you won't hear any complaints,' answered Mr Smith.

'Yer sed 'e wasn't comin' back.'

'He isn't.'

'But yer never sed wot it was yer done ter 'im?'

'You'd be surprised!'

'I wunner! Well, 'ere's me guess, any'ow. Wotever yer done ter 'im, nobody won't see that bobby no more!'

'You couldn't have put it more beautifully!' smiled Mr Smith.

This time, Ben smiled, too.

13

Cobwebs

After the departure of Mr Smith—Ben watched him depart
from the doorstep to make certain he had not turned
back—Ben gave his attention to breakfast, and the change
of occupation was so comforting that he decided to concen-
trate on it and, for the time being, to exclude less pleasing
matters from his thoughts. It was not easy. As he sat at
the kitchen table filling himself with bread and margarine
and marmalade and tea—the fare was simple but there
was plenty of it—he kept on glancing towards the door
in case the monnertrocity should suddenly appear. The
Stacher and the Thing had now merged in Ben's mind into
this new single menace, and if it came, Ben promised, it
would get the teapot in its face. It was just unfortunate
that the kitchen door would not close, and that the slightest
draught or movement swung it to and fro, about an inch
at a time. Then the vision of Sammy lying dead in the
cellar was hard to dismiss. Cheese or pineapple might have
done it, or a chocolate ice sitting on a pancake. Ben had
never had a chocolate ice sitting on a pancake, or even

seen one, but being of an original turn of mind he had always thought the combination would be intriguing. Marmalade did not stand high as a gloom-queller.

Still, judged comparatively, breakfast proved a pleasant occasion, and he drew it out to make it last as long as it could. And when at last it was over, he felt a little more able to contemplate the day ahead of him, with its first high light—or low light—at 10.30 a.m.

'Well, 'ow do we stand nah?' he asked aloud.

Immediately afterwards he wished he had not asked it aloud. Instinctively he had glanced towards the floor at his feet for the companion cat that was not there. For an instant he felt sick, and wondered whether he were going to bring his marmalade up. But it survived the dangerous moment, stayed where it was intended, and was forgotten as Ben answered his own question—but this time not aloud.

How did he stand? What progress, backwards or forwards, had been made in his situation since he had last gone into conference with himself?

Item, on the debit side, Sammy was dead. That, in Ben's summing up, came first. The death of the cat had affected him personally far more than the death of the man on the seat, 'orrerble though that was, or the death of the man on the cellar floor. That was 'orrerble, too, though in a different way. He had not been present at the occasion, so had been spared that, but the death of his predecessor in the role of caretaker had a special significance for him, since what had happened to the first caretaker might so easily happen to the second! Or were they the first and second? Maybe they were the third and fourth! Not a very nice thought, that. He hastily put it aside.

Item, also on the debit side, the monnertrocity. Or was that wholly on the debit side? Convinced, without positive proof, that the Stacher and the Thing were now the Monnertrocity, that reduced the enemy by one. Yes, that certainly was a point in the Monnertrocity's favour. He couldn't suddenly come upon you from both ends of a passage. You only had to keep your eye on one door—though, true, he might choose the other! But bad as a Stacher and a Thing were, a Monnertrocity in Ben's conception was infinitely wuss. And particularly a Monnertrocity who slooshed along like a wet night in a dark alley, and who killed cats.

Coming to the credit side, there was the item of the bogus bobby. Here was an incident which might have trapped Ben into catastrophe, and indeed was designed with a view to that possibility, but instead it had ended in increased prestige! This morning's conversation with Mr Smith had proved to Ben that he had fooled the fooler. It was a pity he had to keep his victory to himself. It would have been pleasant to crow about it. 'Yer thort yer was smart, old cock, didn't yer? Well, see, I was smarter!' Well, perhaps a time would come when he would be able to take Mr Smith and his pals down a peg or two, and show 'em that they weren't the only clever ones!

No, by golly, they weren't! Because what about the lady, too? Mr Smith had spotted her, but Ben had put him off with a yarn. Fooled him twice over. 'I wunner,' reflected Ben, 'if I'm quite sich a mug, arter orl?'

Final item—final, at least, of those now considered—was the advance information concerning the impending visit at half-past ten. Which side of the ledger should that go on? Well, that was how you looked at it. Whatever happened at half-past ten was not going to be a picnic. On the other hand, it would be something definite, and that alone would be a relief after all the unsettling occur- rences in which he had so far not actually participated. Things merely heard, things only seen through keyholes, bogus interviews that were merely preparation for realities to come—these had hitherto been his fate. Now reality for him was about to begin, and he meant to try and make the most out of it, and to learn the most from it. Yes, ten-thirty, whatever it brought, should go down on the credit side.

He took from his pocket the little packet Mr Smith had given into his temporary charge, and eyed it speculatively. A pity about all that sealing-wax! If he opened the packet, as he longed to do, the broken seals would give the show away and he would immediately be suspected, and bang would go all the misplaced confidence in himself he was trying to build up. Of course, there was the odd chance that the contents of the packet would reveal information worth the risk. He doubted, however, whether Mr Smith would have trusted him quite to this extent, and any false move now might prevent him from obtaining the full information he was after.

And so Ben resisted temptation, and replaced the packet unopened in his pocket.

'It might even be another of 'is blinkin' bobby tricks,' he thought, 'with nothink in it bar a piece o' soap! And 'e might of sed ter the agent wot's goin' ter call, if the seals is broke send 'im up ter 'is room and I'll deal with 'im nex' time I come, like them other caretaikers, but if the seals ain't broke 'e's okay, and 'e'll do wot yer tell 'im.'

Yes, and what was *that* going to be? His mind harped back to Mr Smith's precise words: 'Be ready to assist him in any way he may require. And when I say any way, I mean any way. Do you get that?'

Ben had got it.

Well, how was he going to fill the time before the acid test? He was tired of thinking. Thinking was something like walking. You couldn't go on for ever. You got tired after a bit, and if you were walking you sat down, and if you were thinking you shut down. But the idea of doing nothing, often so attractive, did not appeal to Ben in the kitchen of No. 19 Billiter Road. If he did nothing he would start thinking again, and he had got as far as thought would take him. His mind was like a train that had reached the buffers. If it were set once more in motion it would just push and get nowhere. So now he tried to find some simple, peaceful occupation—a nice one that would remind him of home, like. Not that Ben had had any home for many a long year. And as he gazed round the kitchen, it suddenly gave him his answer.

'You could do with a lick and a polish couldn't yer?' he said. 'Let's 'ave a go at the cobbiwebs!'

He found the necessary weapons in a cupboard, and began the attack with a long broom. At first he found the work a little disappointing, for as the filmy conglomerations came festooning down, frequently making their landing on his upturned face, he felt a mutual sympathy with both sides in the conflict. It was not merely that he disliked the taste of mouthfuls of cobwebs, but he felt for the cobwebs themselves, or for their disturbed inhabitants. These cobwebs were their homes—they knew no others—and after they had established their claims by long squatting, up came a bristling thing without any notice, and bing! their home was gone!

''Oo'd like it?' he enquired of one of the displaced inhabitants, a fellow all legs and no body. 'I expeck yer was comforble up there. Sorry, mate!'

But presently, as the battle grew hotter, he overcame his initial sympathy, and began to take pride in the improved appearance of the kitchen. He did not know Carlisle's definition of dirt as matter displaced, but he did realise that matter had to be displaced if the dirt was required to go elsewhere, and he had no doubt that, in due course, such of the worried population as survived would emigrate to become the pioneers of new empires.

He was endeavouring to reach the top of a very tall dresser by standing on one of the kitchen chairs when an ominous crack gave its warning too late. His broom swooped upwards while he swooped downwards, and for a few moments the kitchen became a revolving sphere. When the revolutions ceased he found himself, very obviously, on the floor entangled in the chair.

He did not move for a little while. You always have to wait a bit to find out if you are dead. When he found out he was not, he disentangled himself and sat up to explore for lesser damage. Surprise and relief intermingled. The chair was broken, but he was still whole. Fate did you a good turn sometimes—to make up for all the bad ones.

Where was the broom? He and the chair had been accounted for, but the broom seemed still to be missing. It couldn't have swooped up to the top of the dresser and stayed, could it? It was a wide flat top, the portion nearest the wall concealed from sight from the floor. You'd have to get on a chair to see it, and Ben wasn't going to do that. Nor, he discovered a moment later, was there any need. It had swooped along the unseen top and come down at the other end. There was the handle, sticking out from the wall along the floor by the wide bottom part of the dresser, the part that had drawers in. Might as well pick it up, after Ben had picked himself up, though he wasn't going to do no more cobwebs. He'd call it a day.

He moved to the spot where the broom lay and bent down to pick it up. Something white was under the broom end. What was it? Bit o' paiper. Yus, bit o' paiper. If there wasn't nothink on it, he'd keep it for the next time he wrote to the Lord Mayor.

Must of come dahn from the top. There wasn't no paiper there afore, that he'd lay to. See, he'd swep' that spot, so he knew. Yus, the broom must of brought it dahn when it was wooshing acrost. Looked a bit dusty. Wunner 'ow long it 'ad been up there? But that wasn't the only reason the paper was not suitable for the Lord Mayor. There was already writing on it.

'Let's 'ave a squint,' thought Ben, and took it to the light. ''Allo! Wot's this?'

On the paper was written, in pencil:

'I'd better not see you again. Too damn risky. But I'll get this in the post the next chance I have to slip out, because now I can tell you all you want, and all what's going on here. My God, it's more than we thought! After you've read this, I think you'll agree with me that you'd better give this place a wide berth until' . . .

109

And there it broke off.

Ben read it through three times, and then sat down on one of the surviving kitchen chairs to think about it.

Who had written it? One could only guess, but Ben's guess was the former caretaker. All right. Say it was the caretaker. Never mind if it wasn't. Say it was. Who had he written it *to*? One could only guess again, and this was a harder puzzle to solve, but a disturbing answer suggested itself, and suggested itself in a disturbing way. A vision of the man at the other end of the park seat came to him. Came of its own accord, like. He didn't harp back to it. It came forward at him, and he tried to push it away. He tried to push it away because he didn't like it. He didn't like it at all. See, if this was him, and the other was the other—well, both of 'em was dead, wasn't they?

And this would mean that what he had in his hand was part of a letter from a dead man to a dead man. 'Oo'd never got it, no'ow! No, it wasn't nice.

Why hadn't he got it? Well, that one was easy! He hadn't got it because it hadn't been sent. All right. Why hadn't it been sent? Easy again. It hadn't been sent because it hadn't been finished. All right, again. Why hadn't it been finished? Because—because—well, that would mean an interruption, wouldn't it? Someone had come along. Who?

Now another vision made an ugly smudge in Ben's mind. A vague vision, but bearing an identity not in the least vague. It was the vision of the Monnertrocity, and its effect was so alarming that Ben swung round in his chair and shot an anxious glance towards the door. No one was there, but in his imagination he heard the soft echo of those crunching feet . . . as the writer of the letter might have heard them . . . And then, what would he do? The caretaker? Leap on the dresser, and toss the paper over the top?

And now Ben did hear a sound, and he stuffed the paper quickly in his pocket. It was a soft tapping, and it came from the back door.

14

Overture to 10.30

Who now? What new character was about to be added to the growing list? New it must be, for it could not be the Monnertrocity, already somewhere on the premises, or the agent and his client, who would not tap at the back door but ring at the front, and it was not yet half-past ten. Mr Smith could be ruled out because he had a latchkey.

Ben waited for the tap to be repeated, and when the repetition came he decided to wait for just one more. No further repetition sounding, life began to grow brighter again. Whoever had come had given up, and gone.

Still, you wanted to make quite sure, so after counting thirty very slowly Ben tiptoed from the kitchen to the back door and cautiously opened it. The lady who had called on the previous night stood outside. Mug, not to have thought of it!

'Corse! It's you!' gulped Ben.

'I thought you weren't coming,' she answered. Her voice was anxious but relieved. 'Is it all right to come in?'

Steadying himself, Ben replied, 'Well, yus. But we gotter be careful—and we ain't got much time!'

'How long?'

''Arf past ten.'

'You mean we've got till then?'

'That's right, miss.'

She gave a quick glance at her wrist-watch.

'That gives us twenty minutes. Enough to finish the conversation we couldn't finish last night.' She slipped inside the dark passage, and Ben closed the door. 'Where shall we talk?'

'Kitching,' said Ben, and led the way.

She glanced around curiously when they were in the room, and her eyes rested on the overturned broken chair, but she made no comment. Instead she asked,

'Do you know if I was seen leaving here?'

'Yer was,' nodded Ben.

'I was afraid so.'

'But I put that right.'

'How do you mean?'

'Well, see, the bloke wot engaiged me—I told yer abart 'im—'e come agine this mornin', and 'e sez wot abart it, so I tells 'im yer'd jest come ter the wrong address, and 'e swallered it 'ole.'

'That was clever of you!'

'Well, I wouldn't say that. I'd almost given up when it come ter me. I 'ope 'e didn't see yer come jest now?'

'No, I've been terribly careful. Was the man who left here a little while ago the man you've mentioned?'

'Oh! Yer saw 'im?'

'Not distinctly.'

'That's the one. P'r'aps I'll tell yer a bit more abart

113

'im, but fust yer goin' ter tell *me* somethink, aincher? Wot we was interrupted abart last night. Corse,' he added, 'afore we really gets goin', you gotter know I ain't a wrong 'un and I gotter know you ain't one. That's right, ain't it?'

She smiled. 'Do you think I'm a wrong 'un?'

'If yer wants the fack,' he answered, 'I'd bet nex' Sunday's dinner yer ain't.'

'Thank you. I'm quite sure now you're not a wrong 'un—'

'Oi! Not so loud, if yer don't mind!' She looked startled, and he quickly reassured her. 'Okay, nobody's 'earin' us, but wot I meant was yer gotter be careful wot yer say abart me if anybody *does*. See, I'm s'posed ter be a wrong 'un, and if it's fahnd aht I ain't I'm a gorner! Yus, but drop me fer a bit and let's 'ear wot brort yer 'ere, and wot yer want, and 'oo this Mr Remington is—'

'Remington?'

'The bloke yer was arskin' abart.'

'Bretherton.'

'Oh, was it? Okay. Bretherton. 'Oo is 'e?' A sudden idea came to Ben. 'Is 'e comin' 'ere terday with the agent?'

Now a new look came into her face. A troubled look. It troubled Ben.

'I wish—he were!' Then she gave herself a little shake, as though to dismiss the sadness in her voice, and when she spoke again it was with the hardness which Ben had noticed at the beginning of their first interview 'No. He is not coming here. You don't know, then?'

'Don't know what, miss?' muttered Ben, struggling not to know. For his mind was becoming too perceptive for comfort. There is a lot to be said, at times, for ignorance.

'You don't know why he couldn't be coming here?' she asked, watching him closely.

'Well, p'r'aps that's one o' the things yer goin' ter tell me?' was Ben's evasive response.

She nodded, and suddenly sat down on the nearest chair. Ben recognised that abrupt need to sit. He often got it. It was when your knees went weak.

'Yes. It is,' she said. 'He—Mr Bretherton—he is dead.'

('Wait for it!' thought Ben.)

'He was murdered yesterday afternoon. You—you didn't know anything about that?'

'Well, I knew abart the murder, miss,' answered Ben, carefully.

'Oh! You did!'

'But not 'oo 'e was.'

'How did you know about the murder?'

'I'll tell yer in a minit, but p'r'aps yer'd better finish your bit fust.'

'Very well. I'm trusting you. He was murdered on a park seat. Have you seen the morning papers?'

Ben shook his head.

'There's a photograph. Somebody took it just before—it happened. Mr Bretherton was on one end of the seat, and the man who is believed to have killed him was on the other.' She paused, and then added, 'I came here because I thought the man might be here.'

'Oh!' murmured Ben. 'Did yer?'

'Yes.'

'I see.' He didn't quite. 'But when yer called larst night yer 'adn't seed the pickcher. Or did some'un show it to yer?'

'No, I hadn't seen it,' she answered. 'I didn't call because

115

of the picture. What I meant was that I thought the murderer might be here, or I might learn some news of him.'

'Ah, that's more like it! See, it mightn't of bin the bloke in the pickcher at all. As a matter of fack, miss, I 'appens ter know as it wasn't.'

'You do?' she exclaimed, in surprise.

'I orter. And now, as yer trustin' me, I'm goin' ter trust you. I'm the bloke.'

Her surprise changed to utter astonishment. She stared at him, speechless.

'The reason yer don't reckernise me is 'cos I've 'ad me fice chainged,' went on Ben. 'It's bin chainged by the chap wot took the photo, and 'e took the photo 'cos 'e wanted ter put the blime on me fer wot 'e done 'iself—'

'*What*!' she gasped.

'That's right, miss. 'E done it. It was the chap with the mustache wot brort me 'ere arter I see 'im do it. Fust 'e tikes the photer and then 'e gives me a dose o' dope, and when I come to I'm 'ere and 'e sez I done it meself! 'E got me proper, but I ain't stayin' on 'ere on'y fer that. See, I'm goin' ter git me own back on 'im and find aht wot 'is gime is, oh, yus, there's a gime on 'ere orl right, wich is why I'm pertendin' ter be a wrong 'un, like I sed, see, if I didn't I wouldn't learn nothink, would I, it'd be the finish, and—'

'Wait!' she interrupted. 'You're going too fast! I can't take it all in!'

'Sime 'ere. It gits yer dizzy.'

'Do you really mean what you're saying? That you were doped and brought here—'

'That's right. I woke up in a bed upstairs, and there was Mr Smith, any'ow that's wot 'e calls 'iself, the one

116

'oo did it, there 'e was watchin' of me and tellin' me wot
I 'ad ter do.'

'What was that?'

'Eh?' Ben jerked his head round. 'Where?'

'I meant what did you have to do?'

'Oh, I git yer. This plice mikes yer jumpy. Wot did I 'ave
ter do? Lummy, it's a mouthful, but the start of it was I
'ad to be the caretaiker o' this 'ouse or be 'anded over ter
the pleece, see, when I was subconshus 'e fixed me fingerprints on the knife. 'E'd worked the 'ole thing aht from
Adam to Eve. If yer git me.'

'But this is terrible!'

'Yer ain't 'eard nothink yet!'

'There's some more?'

'You ain't 'eard abart the Monnertrocity, there's one
somewhere abart, or the caretaiker afore me, 'e's dead, or
the cat wot they killed, too. Nice cat, that was. We got
quite chummy. Or abart the bobby wot called 'ere arter
you did larst night, or did you call arter 'im, no, 'e called
arter you, lummy, yer gits so mixed up yer don't know if
it's Monday or Friday—'

'Please, don't go so fast!' she begged. 'Did you say the
police had been here?'

'Not the real pleece, miss, it was a bogious one,' replied
Ben, trying to slow his pace. But once he had started,
everything had poured out of him as if he had suddenly
sprung a leak where he talked, and he had found it difficult
to stop. 'See, they wanted ter find aht if I'd give 'em away
if the pleece *did* call, but luckerly I got on ter it withaht
'im knowin', so nah they think I'm the proper goods!' He
paused at a thought. ''Ave you bin ter the pleece, miss?'

'No,' she replied.

'I reckon that's jest as well—on'y why not?'

'I'll tell you when I finish my story. Please go on with yours.'

'Okay, on'y ain't we tellin' 'em in the wrong order?'

'That doesn't matter. Wait a moment, though. Why are you glad I haven't been to the police?'

'Well, it's like this, see, on'y I ain't sure as I can expline. Sometimes the pleece is the best blokes ter find a thing aht, but sometimes they ain't, 'cos when they comes the birds is flown, if yer git me, or else yer carn't git nothink aht of 'em. Well, I sizes up that this is one o' the times, and the way things 'as worked aht I'm orl set ter find aht wot the pleece carn't. Is that too fast or do yer foller it?'

'I see what you mean.'

'Thank Gawd yer do, 'cos me bones tells me I'm right, and I ain't no good at puttin' things not if they ain't simple. There's a big gime on, with brines be'ind it, and they'll smell a bobby comin' if 'e's a mile orf, yus, and when the bobby did git 'ere 'e wouldn't learn nothink aht o' me 'cos they'd say I done it and I'd be 'ad. But I was tellin' yer. Where was I upter? Oh, yus, 'ere's the next thing. At 'arf-past ten the agent's comin' to show some'un over the 'ouse—'

'Do you mean Wavell?' she interrupted sharply.

'Yus, that's the nime?'

'I know him.'

'Yer do?'

'I've worked for him! That's one reason I'm here.'

'Oh! Well, in that caise yer'd think 'e'd be orl right—'

'On the contrary, I stopped working for him because he wasn't all right! Half-past ten? Then we've only got a few more minutes. He mustn't find me here. He'd recognise me. Go on, go on! What more do you know about him?'

'I don't know nothink, except wot I gotter do.'

'What's that?'

'I gotter give 'im a packet. This 'un.' He took it from his pocket. 'I'd 'ave a look inside on'y they'd know if I broke the seals. Arter that I gotter go up ter the top room and waite till they go, excep' if the agent wants me ter 'elp 'im.'

'Help him?'

'Yus.'

'In what way?'

'I dunno. 'E'll tell me, I s'pose. But I gotter do it, wotever it is. Them's me instruckshuns.'

'Who gave them to you? The man you call Mr Smith?'

'That's right.'

'The man you say killed Mr Bretherton?'

'That's the one. 'E give em to me this mornin', and if I'm good and do orl I'm told I'm s'posed ter be onter a good thing. That's 'is baite like. Do wot I sez and yer'll 'ave a nice prize. Yus, and with a bloke like that, see me gittin' it! Any'ow, them's me orders, and it looks ter me like bein' a nice cup o' tea! Yus, but 'arf a mo',' went on Ben, as she began to speak again, 'there's somethink else, yus, I better tell yer this.'

'Is it important?' she asked almost impatiently, with a swift glance at her wrist-watch.

'I reckon it is, miss,' answered Ben. 'Leastwise, it might be, but then yer doesn't orlways know not till arterwards, do yer? There's a button on the floor. "'Allo!" yer sez, and picks it up. P'r'aps it'll 'ang a man, or p'r'aps it's jest orf the milkman's trahsers. Yer never knows not till arterwards.'

'We'd better not waste time over it,' she said.

'Over wot?'

'The button—but you can show it to me, if you like.'

'There ain't no button.'

'Didn't you say—?'

'Ah, I was speakin' wot's called—wot's called—I've fergot. Illierstrashun like, is that it? Any'ow, wot I fahnd wer'n't on the floor, it was up on the top o' that there dresser, see, I was sweepin' it with a broom, that's 'ow the chair fell over, and dahn it come.'

'The chair?'

'Eh? No, I come dahn with the chair, the other come dahn orf the top o' the dresser, like I sed. The chair was on the bottom bit where it sticks aht.'

'*What* came down from the top—?'

'Well, I'm tellin' yer, miss. It was a bit o' paiper. Well, 'ere it is. See if yer can mike anythink aht of it? Looks like ter me as if—'

The word 'if' came out of Ben's mouth at exactly half-past ten, and with the most inconsiderate promptitude, the front-door bell rang.

15

10.30

'Gawd, that's torn it!' gulped Ben.

'Quick!' whispered the lady, and snatching the paper from Ben's hand she ran to the kitchen door.

But she stopped at Ben's hoarse voice.

'Oi, miss! Arf a mo'!'

'What?'

'Better waite till I lets 'em in afore yer goes aht.'

'That's true.'

'And they may leave some'un ahtside arter they comes in. Watchin' like.'

'You mean Mr Smith?'

'Most likely 'im, though there's others, as well.'

She considered swiftly, then nodded.

'I'll be careful. Go up! They're ringing again.' She moved out into the passage. 'Better be quick!'

He followed her out, but paused at the foot of the cold stone basement stairs to look at her. She had moved no more herself.

'I ain't 'eard wot *you* gotter tell me yet,' he muttered.

'I know,' she answered, 'and you must.'

'When?'

'I'll find a way.' Knocking began. 'We can't talk any more now. They'll have the door down. Later.'

Trying to compose himself, Ben mounted the basement stairs. Half-way up he stopped and turned, but the lady either had gone or was standing in too deep a shadow for Ben's quick glance to pick her out. He would have given much for these new callers to have been five minutes late. It would have been helpful if he could have been armed with her knowledge as well as his own. For all he could say, when she came back again it might be too late. Still, Ben had long learned that you had to deal with a situation as it was, not as you wished it were, and that to spend your time wishing was no way to ease your burdens. On the contrary, it merely added further defeats to the already disturbing score.

So now he suddenly accelerated, and he arrived at the front door before a fourth summons could occur. Opening it, he saw the two expected men standing on the doorstep. One, the larger, glowered at him.

'Been asleep?' he barked.

'I'm 'ere now,' replied Ben.

'Do you know how long you've kept us waiting?'

'It's a long way dahn orl them stairs.'

'Oh, you were up at the top?'

'Yus, and I've got rhoomertism in me 'ip.'

'It sounded as though you came up from the basement,' remarked the man, as he stepped in, followed by his companion. 'You weren't down there?'

In case sounds had been heard below, Ben thought it best to offer some explanation. His intention to tell lies was no firmer than his determination not to be caught out in any.

'Well, see, I come dahn with a cupple o' brooms in each 'and,' he said, 'and so I carried on fust to the kitching.'

The other man now spoke. He was of a very different type. His figure was delicate and slight, and he had a small beard. His voice was educated and refined.

'It would certainly,' he observed, with a smile, 'be difficult to open a door with two brooms in each hand.'

'Eh?'

'Do you always work with four?'

'Let's get on with it, let's get on with it!' snapped the first man, and then suddenly glanced half-apologetically at the other, who was looking at him rather curiously. 'Terrible lot to do lately—feeling a bit short-tempered this morning, but never mind, never mind!' He turned back to Ben. 'It's your fault, you know, for having kept us on the doorstep so long. Now, let me see. You're the new caretaker here, of course, aren't you?'

Behind his overbearing manner Ben now noticed traces of nervousness.

'That's right,' answered Ben.

'Jones, isn't it?'

'That's right. And your'n'll be Wavell?'

'I am Mr Wavell.' He spoke a little stiffly. 'And naturally, Jones, I have to report on your behaviour, so of course you will see that you give me no cause for complaint.'

'Since we are covering introductions,' added the alleged house-hunter, 'my name is Black. So now we all know each other, do we not?'

Mr Black still wore his faint smile, as though now he were amused at something else, not this time brooms.

123

'Okay,' said Ben, and then thought it would be a good idea to try and impress his visitors with his efficiency. 'But as I'm new on me job, 'ow abart lettin' me be sure I'm dealin' with the right parties?' Mr Wavell's eyebrows went up. 'Wot I mean, sir, is that ain't there a list or somethink I orter see afore showin' yer over the 'ouse like?'

'A rightly cautious fellow,' commented Mr Black, and then threw a glance at the agent as though to see how he was taking it.

'Well, see, I 'as ter be,' replied Ben, ''cos it wasn't Mr Wavell 'oo engaiged me, and the chap wot did lef' me in charge o' the property.'

'You certainly appear to be doing that very thoroughly,' returned Mr Wavell, his tone less complimentary than his words.

'Then I 'opes yer'll put it in that there report,' said Ben, and felt rightly that he had scored.

'It shall undoubtedly be mentioned, yes, undoubtedly,' replied the agent, 'but I also want to be able to report some progress.'

'I ain't stoppin' yer goin' over the plice.'

'No, quite so—but—er—by the way, have you anything for me before we start?'

The question was asked casually, to cover its importance.

'That's right, sir. And yer shall 'ave it when I seen that list.'

Here Mr Black interposed again. He seemed, for the most part, a silent man.

'I have the list myself,' he said, and taking it from his pocket he handed it to Ben.

It was a large sheet headed 'Wavell & Son,' and it

contained a neat typed list of some dozen houses. No. 19, Billiter Road, was the fourth house down. From Ben's brief glance the description appeared to have somewhat over-stated the desirable premises' attractions.

'That's okay,' nodded Ben, and handed the list back.

'And now for what *you* have for *me*?' said the agent. Ben fished in his pocket, and produced the sealed packet.

"Ere it is,' he answered. 'Jest as I got it.'

Mr Black, now looking slightly curious again, glanced from one to the other as the packet changed hands. But he made no comment, and a short silence ensued, during which Mr Wavell held the packet as though uncertain just what to do with it.

'It's jest as I got it orf Mr Smith,' Ben repeated. 'The seals ain't broke.'

All at once the agent woke up.

'Of course not, of course not,' he exclaimed, busily. 'Why should they be?' He turned to Mr Black. 'Just something I left behind the last time I saw Mr Smith. Nothing of importance, nothing at all.'

'Mr Smith being?' queried Mr Black.

What, didn't he know?

'Eh? Oh, the owner of the property. At least—yes, of course, of course. And a nice price he's asking for it? But he may reduce it, he may reduce it. Well, let's get cracking. Let's go down.'

'Basement first?' Mr Black enquired.

'Yes. Bottom upwards, eh? Yes, I think so.'

Once more Mr Wavell seemed uncertain of his next step, for he did not move at once towards the basement stairs. Breaking a further short pause, Ben put a leading question.

'Will you be wanting me, sir?' he asked the agent.

'Ah—will I—? No, I don't—wait a moment, wait a moment. Yes, yes, after all. Just show Mr Black the drawing-room, will you, Jones, while I—the door on the right, Mr Black. I'll join you in a moment.'

Ben saw behind the move. Mr Wavell wanted an opportunity to open the packet privately, and afterwards, perhaps, he would be a little clearer in his mind. A nasty bit of work Mr Wavell was, Ben decided. A very nasty bit of work, and he recalled that the lady, whose name even yet he had not learned, had warned him of this. She'd worked for him, and she knew. What was her work? And what had Mr Wavell done that had caused her to leave him? If only there had been time to hear her full story! And if only the packet had not been sealed, so Ben might have learned its contents!

These thoughts ran round and round his mind while he conducted Mr Black into the room which the agent had indicated. It was the one room on that floor which contained any furniture, and Ben had not been in it since his original investigation of the house on the evening before. While his mind was busy, he watched Mr Black out of the corner of his eye, and although Mr Black gazed round dutifully at the couch and the armchair and the gate-legged table with the blue china vase on it, he himself seemed to be watching Ben. 'If 'e's thinkin' I'm a rum sort o' care-taker,' reflected Ben, ''e's sed it!'

Mr Black made a remark after a few moments which suggested Ben's guess was a good one.

'I have been trying to make out where you come from,' he said. 'There is something almost foreign in your appearance—I once had a French manservant who looked

126

something like you—but your voice is definitely—well, insular.'

Ben had no idea what insular meant, but whatever it was he felt it must be wrong, and he suddenly remembered that he was making no effort to change his usual voice to fit his unusual face.

'That would be becorse me father and me mother was so dif'rent,' he answered, carefully.

'H'm. Well, there may be something in that.'

'There is, sir. When a black cat and a white cat matches up, that's 'ow you get a black cat with a white 'ead.'

'Indeed? I am learning.'

'This is a nice room, sir, is it not?' said Ben, to change the subject.

'That is a matter of opinion. I cannot say I think very much of the view,' responded Mr Black.

'Oh, them roofs. Well, see, that's bomb damage, but it all gits covered up in the summer, wot with things growin' and that.'

'I understood you only took this job yesterday.'

'Eh?'

'Perhaps you have not had much time yet to tidy up? But I should have thought, if you work with four brooms, you would have finished the whole house by now.'

What did that mean? Ben followed Mr Black's eyes, and suddenly knew what he meant. Mr Black was looking at the broken vase at the foot of the curtain, and the hammer.

'Will that damage have to figure in Mr Wavell's report?'

'That wasn't done by me,' muttered Ben.

'No? By whom, if one may ask?'

Before Ben could formulate any reply, the agent came bustling into the room. He emanated a false brightness which did not deceive Ben. 'That packet wer'n't no nerve tonic,' decided Ben. ''E's still worried!'

'Well, well, here we are!' exclaimed Mr Wavell breezily, like one bringing good news. 'How do you like it, Mr Black? But perhaps you'd better wait for your verdict until you've seen the whole place. Let me see, the basement, wasn't it? We were going to start there, and work upwards.' He swung round to Ben. 'We won't be needing you any more, Jones. You can go up to your room, where I've no doubt you have work to do.' Twisting round to Mr Black again: 'I'll follow you, Mr Black. We must get moving. I'll follow you.'

With a slight shrug Mr Black left the room, but Mr Wavell lingered by Ben till Mr Black was in the hall. Then a quick whisper tickled Ben's ear.

'*Stay here! I may want you! Come if I call!*'

Before Ben could reply, if reply were expected, Mr Wavell had slid out of the room, and he was alone again.

16

Where's Mr Black?

'Nah wot?' wondered Ben.

It was a question to which he had no answer, and the next four minutes, while by no means the worst he had so far endured in this uncomfortable adventure or was destined to endure before it ended, had a savour of unpleasantness peculiarly their own. At any moment anything might happen, though nothing actually did. In the uncanny silence that followed the fading out of Mr Black's and Mr Wavell's footsteps down the basement stairs, he stood tensely at attention, expecting a shout or a thud or a scream or a shot, or any one of the countless sounds which imply trouble. Ben knew them all! Whichever one occurred would be a call to action. What action? No good arskin' 'im! All he knew was that it wouldn't be any fun.

After the four minutes had run their painful course—to Ben they had seemed more like forty—he decided that it might be a good idea to relax a little. It is exhausting to maintain, for two hundred and forty seconds, the attitude of a sprinter waiting for the starting pistol. Unstiffening himself, he waited another minute, then moved cautiously to the door and poked his head out.

Not a sound came up from below. The hall was oppressively empty. Oppressively? Didn't he want it to be empty? What was it he missed, then? Not the agent or the house-hunter, certainly, for their absence was far preferable to their presence. But he did miss something, and it wasn't the cat this time, either. All at once he got it. He had vaguely hoped he might see the lady. It was not merely her company he would have welcomed, but a sight of her would have reassured him as to her safety. He had left her down in that basement. He prayed she had made her get-away before the new callers had descended. A nuisance they'd gone down! If only they'd gone up instead! Because—well—suppose—?

'Allo! Wot was that? Something at last! Or was it? Blast his imagination! Think of a thing hard enough and you hatch it. Now he was imagining the cry he had been expecting. Lummy, and now he was imagining a distant scuffle. Just the echo of contending bodies. Oi, that's enough, that's enough! Once imagination gets a proper grip on you there's no holding it!

Drawn forward against his will, he left the room and moved towards the basement stairs across the gloomy echoing hall, but as he reached the top of the stairs he drew back quickly at the sound of someone at the bottom.

The someone began to come up, his unwelcome progress marked by the dismal clang of boot on stone. Well, a clang was better than a crunch, for it was the monnertrocity who crunched!

As the hurried steps grew closer Ben retreated to the back room door, and from there watched the answer to his question develop out of the staircase gloom. It was the agent, alone. Mr Wavell looked a little less tidy and far more worried than when he had descended. Reaching the top of the stairs and not seeing Ben for a moment, he lurched towards the front door. Then he stopped abruptly, as though remembering something. Ben guessed as Mr Wavell half-turned and saw him that he was what had suddenly been remembered.

'Oh—you still here?' blinked Mr Wavell fatuously.

'Where else I'd be?' answered Ben.

'What?'

'Didn't yer tell me ter stick arahnd in caise yer wanted me?'

Trying to pull himself together, Mr Wavell nodded.

'That's right, that's right,' he said.

'And yer didn't want me?' went on Ben.

With a vacuous laugh, the agent retorted, 'Well, does it look like it?'

'No, it don't.'

'All right, then.'

'I 'ope so.'

'What's that mean?'

'I'll tell you wot it *does* look like!'

'What?' The monosyllable was snapped out. 'Don't start getting funny!'

'I ain't feelin' funny, guv'nor, no more'n you are! It looks like yer didn't need me ter 'elp yer 'cos yer fahnd yer could do it by yerself.'

'Do what?'

'I've told yer my 'arf. That's the 'arf I want yer ter tell *me*!'

'Here! You're talking nonsense, my man, and I've no time for it!' exclaimed Mr Wavell. 'Good-morning!'

131

He began to move towards the front door again, but his movement was uncertain, and he paused once more at Ben's next question.

'Where's Mr Black?'

'Mr Black?'

'Ain't you never 'eard of 'im?'

'Of course I've—what the deuce has come over you?' The attempt at indignation was not very successful. 'You're the caretaker here, aren't you? All right, then! Stick to your job, and leave others to do theirs.'

'Oh! You jest done a job, then?' enquired Ben, stolidly.

When your companion is more nervous than you are, you acquire a comparative courage.

'Job?' repeated Mr Wavell angrily, and then looked scared at the loudness of his voice.

'Where's Mr Black?'

'If you want to know, he's—he's left.'

'I didn't see him go.'

'I can't help that, can I? And now I'm going myself. If anybody—'

''E ain't gorn,' said Ben.

'I tell you he has!'

'I'd of seed 'im! I bin 'ere orl the time.'

'I see! And so you think that therefore you must have seen him go?'

'I didn't go ter sleep.'

A crafty light illumined Mr Wavell's eye, without beautifying it.

'Mr Black,' said the agent, 'left by the back door.'

'Oh!'

'Satisfied?'

'No.'

'Why not? No, never mind, what the blazes does it matter if you're satisfied or not—'

'You arsked!'

'Very well, then. Why not?'

''Cos why should 'e?'

'Damnation! He was in a hurry!'

'I see,' said Ben. ''E was in such a 'urry 'e 'adn't time ter come up the stairs and go aht the way 'e come in. 'E 'ad ter ketch a trine—'

'As a matter of fact, he had—'

'And so 'e goes aht of the back door wot I locked and kep' the key in me pocket.'

Mr Wavell's eyebrows shot up. 'What! You locked it, you say?'

'That's wot I sed.'

'And—and have the key—'

'No. It's dahnstairs in the door, but yer'd of knowed I couldn't of 'ad it if Mr Black went aht that way.'

The situation could have been more lucidly expressed, but Mr Wavell interpreted it, and suddenly took out a handkerchief to wipe a moist brow.

'Now, listen to me,' he said, with a sort of desperate earnestness. 'If there are things you don't understand about me, there are things I don't understand about *you*! Let's straighten this out a bit. You've already confirmed that you are the caretaker here. I take it that is correct?'

'Orl correck,' agreed Ben.

'Which, being so,' continued Mr Wavell, now beginning to choose his words carefully, 'I take it you have been informed of your duties?'

'I bin told.'

'How much have you been told?'

'Ah!'

'Most informative! One thing might be not to ask questions?'

'Yus, and another might be not ter answer 'em!'

With an ineffective attempt to regain distinction, Mr Wavell stiffened.

'You do know, I suppose, the difference between a man in my position and a man in yours? An agent—a reputable agent—and a caretaker—'

''Ow abart leavin' aht the respertable?'

'What? God bless my soul! All right, then! We will certainly leave out the adjectives, which goes for both of us. Now, then, we'll begin again, and this time I hope keep our minds clear! Frankly I never met anybody like you, and hope I never do again. You were engaged by—er—Mr Smith to do a job. We will not enquire too deeply into the kind of job, but—shall we say—not quite the usual sort of a job?'

'That's okay.'

'And one of your jobs was to give me a packet?'

'Yus.'

'The contents of which you—knew?'

'Eh?'

'Did you know?'

'The seals wasn't broke.'

'I recall that. If they had been, you and I would not be talking together now so—h'm—amicably?' Mr Wavell gave a sudden smile that reminded Ben of sour sugar. If sugar could be sour. Could it? Milk went sour, and then you got cheese. If sugar went sour, saying it could, what—

'Are you listening?' came Mr Wavell's voice, raspingly.

'That's right,' answered Ben, unwinding. 'The seals

wasn't broke and that's mide us amiacal like. Well, wot abart it?'

'What I am trying to say—what I asked you was, even though the seals were not broken, did you know what the packet contained?'

''Ow could I?'

'Mr Smith didn't tell you?'

'No.'

'And you didn't guess?'

'I guessed it was somethink smutty.'

'Meaning—?'

'Well, somethink that the pleece might 'ave thort orf the track, if yer git me.'

'Exactly,' nodded Mr Wavell. 'And so—knowing that— why are you worrying so much about what has happened to Mr Black? If you get *me*?'

'I git yer,' answered Ben. 'Yer mean, 'e ain't gorn.'

'Would that trouble you?'

''E's still 'ere?'

Mr Wavell considered his reply, then said, 'Yes—in a sense.'

'Wot sense?' Ben's heart gave a jump. 'Yer don't mean— jest 'is body like?'

'And if I did?' Mr Wavell thrust his head forward, and suddenly Ben became conscious of his bulging pale blue eyes and rather flabby cheeks; and in the tense little moment that followed, during which the agent stood motionless, he turned into a wax figure in the Chamber of Horrors at Madame Tussaud's, with a label attached to him: 'The Murderer of Mr Black.' And beside him was another figure in a light grey suit, with brown hair and a small moustache, bearing the label: 'The Murderer of Mr Bretherton.' And beside him yet another, the worst of all, with large flat bare feet and an enormous misshapen three-eyed head: 'The Murderer of Seven Caretakers.' And beside him—Ben? . . .

'God above, what are you staring at!' cried Mr Wavell, as something snapped inside him. 'I've had enough of you! I'm going!'

''Arf a mo'!' jerked Ben.

He extended a hand to detain him, and Mr Wavell, misinterpreting the movement through his neurotic condition into one of violence, struck at him. Ben ducked and struck back, and the next instant they were both rolling on the ground in a tussle which neither had intended nor wanted. The agent was the first to regain his feet. When Ben started rolling he generally went on for a long while. Limping to the door, his face contorted with pain, Mr Wavell seized the handle and pulled the door open. But he did not go out. For a moment he stood transfixed, a wax figure once more, while Ben stopped rolling and began to get up. Then the door was swiftly closed again, and Mr Wavell backed to the basement staircase, his eyes fixed on the door as he backed.

Ben's imagination, which often outstripped reality and was now working hard, conjured up a vision of the corpse of Mr Black mounting the front steps. The agent's expression of fascinated fear suited the conception. Ben found himself watching the door with him.

'Some'un comin'?' muttered Ben.

Mr Wavell did not reply immediately. There was no need to. It soon became obvious that someone was coming, and any lingering doubt was dissipated by the sound of the bell. 'Ow Ben 'ated that bell!

'Get rid of her!' whispered Mr Wavell, no longer an

antagonist but imploring co-operation. 'Get rid of her! I'm not here! I've never been here. I'm not—'

And then he wasn't, for he vanished down the basement stairs, ending at the bottom with a crash.

'Nah, listen!' said Ben to himself. 'I ain't goin' ter 'urry this. I gotter git me breath back, ain't I? Orl right, then! I ain't goin' ter 'urry it, see?'

He did not hurry. He let the bell ring twice. Then as he went to open the door his anxiety all at once changed to relief. 'She,' he'd said. She! Well, of course, that would be the lady he had been talking to before Mr Wavell and Mr Black arrived. Mug, again, not to think of it! She'd been hovering around to finish their conversation, and now believed the coast was clear. And Mr Wavell didn't want to meet her because she'd worked for him—didn't she say she had?—yes, of course she did—and she'd found him out.

When he opened the door he saw a hard-eyed woman dressed in black standing before him.

17

Lady No. Two

'This ain't fair,' Ben decided. 'I don't git no warnin'. 'Oo's this 'un? 'Ow am I ter know which side she's on and which side I gotter be on whichever side she is? It ain't fair. Yer don't git no warnin'. It ain't fair.'

And so, lacking any policy, he donned an expression which he hoped would convey nothing until he knew what he wanted to convey; and as the nearest thing it came to was a dead haddock, it fulfilled its purpose.

'Good-morning,' began this latest visitor, stiffly.

'Good-mornin',' replied the dead haddock.

'Can I see Mr Wavell?' she asked.

'Mr 'Oo?' answered Ben.

'Mr Wavell.'

'Oh! Mr Wavell.'

'You know him, of course?'

'Well, see, there's mor'n one.'

'Don't be trying! This is Mr Ernest Wavell. Not the General.'

'Ah! Well, '*e* wouldn't of bin 'ere!'

'Hardly. The Mr Wavell I am talking about is the head of the firm of Wavell and Son, house-agents.'

'Oh! That 'un.'

An expression of exasperation swept across her face. It was not a happy face, which might have endeared it to Ben, for he was drawn to unhappy people. Sort of unnerstood 'em like. But he could not hatch any fondness for this grim, unattractive lady. She wasn't like that other one. Still, corse, yer never knew, did yer? Wot yer saw didn't orlways give yer wot was unnerneath. Same with 'orses. 'Old aht yer 'and ter the gentlest lookin' in the row and ten ter one 'e'd bite yer . . .

'Are you listening?'

'Eh? Yus, that's right, mum,' jerked Ben. 'Wavell and Son. That's right.'

'You do know the firm, then,' said the lady, with thinly veiled irony.

'Well, why wouldn't I?' hedged Ben.

'You certainly ought to if they are agents for this house.' She paused, as though waiting for corroboration. When none came she was forced to put the question. 'They are the agents, are they not?'

'Don't the board say?' replied Ben.

He thought this good, but was proved an optimist.

'There isn't any board,' she answered.

'Oh! Ain't there?'

'You didn't know that?'

'I expeck it's got blowed dahn.'

'I saw no sign of it.'

'I expeck it was took away while they was gettin' another.'

With forced patience, the lady in black enquired whether, when the new board came, it would bear the name of

Wavell and Son. Worn out by her persistence, Ben risked the admission that it would do so, though it occurred to him that if there was no board now there probably would never be one. This was not a house that advertised itself.

'So let's get back to where we started from,' said the lady. 'I understand that Mr Wavell is not at his office—as a matter of fact I rang up to find out—so I thought he might be here.'

'I see, mum. They tole yer 'e was 'ere.'

She hesitated, then shook her head, admitting the truth rather grudgingly.

'No—they didn't tell me,' she responded. 'The girl did not seem to know. She just said he was out with a client, and I was given to understand that there was a long list of houses to be visited.'

'I see,' nodded Ben, 'and they give yer the list and yer callin' at the lot?'

'Certainly not.'

'Oh! Then wot mide yer choose this 'un, mum—?'

'*Will* you stop asking questions and answer mine?' she interrupted angrily. 'Do you think I propose to stand here listening to your nonsense? Is Mr Wavell here, or isn't he?'

Further postponement being impossible, Ben tossed in his mind. 'Eads 'e is, tails 'e ain't. The imaginary coin came down heads.

'' E ain't,' said Ben.

After all, why obey a coin that wasn't here, either?

The lady frowned. Her expression was sceptical, but she seemed uncertain of her next move. It took her a few seconds to decide, and when she spoke again her tone was rather more conciliatory.

'That's a pity—I hoped he was,' she said. 'You know

him, of course? If this house is on his firm's books, I expect
he has been here. You *are* the caretaker?'

'That's right.'

'Mr Wavell engaged you, I dare say?' Leave that one,
unless she repeated it. 'Did he?'

Lummy, why didn't she go? He wanted to find out what
was happening in the basement. Of course it wouldn't be no
picnic, finding out wouldn't, but it had to be done, and if
she kept him here much longer . . . 'Allo! Wot was that? . . .
'Did he?'

'Eh? 'Oo did wot? Oh, yus. I mean no. 'E didn't engaige
me—not Mr Wavell didn't.'

'Who did engage you?'

'Some'un else did.'

'Naturally, if Mr Wavell didn't! The owner?'

'That's right.'

'Who is the owner? What's his—?'

She stopped in the middle of the sentence, and looked
beyond Ben's shoulder. Had she heard something, too?

'Look 'ere, mum,' he said, earnestly, 'I'm the caretaiker
'ere, like I told yer, but I ain't bin engaiged ter give pertick-
lers, you better git them orf the agent, see, I on'y 'as ter
show people rahnd wot's interested in the 'ouse—'

'Then suppose you show *me* round?' she interrupted,
tartly. 'I happen to be rather interested in this house myself.'

Making one last effort against this determined woman,
Ben replied,

''Ave yer got a norder, mum? I ain't supposed ter show
no one rahnd not if they ain't got a norder.'

'I don't need any order, thank you,' she retorted. 'Perhaps,
since you are so particular, it might be a good idea for
you to ask who I am?'

'Oh! Then 'oo are yer?'

'I am Mrs Wavell, Mr Wavell's wife. Now may I come in? You say Mr Wavell is not here, but *someone* is! I heard them below those stairs a few moments ago, and whoever they are I am quite certain of one thing—they will be more satisfactory to talk to than you are!'

She began to push past him, then paused at his expression.

'You seem surprised,' she said.

'Well, mum—yer didn't tell me,' muttered Ben.

'That may have been because of your most extraordinary attitude when you opened the door to me! What is going on in this house? Would you like to inform me, or must I find out for myself?'

Ben gave up.

'Yer can please yerself, mum,' he answered. 'I ain't stoppin' yer.'

And why, after all, should he? This was something new—something not in the original picture—and he could not be expected to handle it! Let her go down and find her husband! If she did, perhaps Ben would learn something in the shindy!

But as she resumed her way to the head of the stairs a new thought—a new reason for detaining her—came into his mind. He didn't like her, that was a fact, but she was a lady, and you had to look after ladies, didn't you? You know—whoever they were. And if she didn't know what was going on in the house any more than Ben did, and might bump into a corpse at any moment, well, she ought to be warned like, oughtn't she?

So he called out. ''Arf a mo'!' but it had no effect. Mrs Wavell either did not hear or chose not to hear, and descended the stone stairs with a determination there was no combating. Very well, then. If a little too tardily, Ben had done his best, and she must take the consequences. And so, incidentally, must Mr Wavell, if that unhappy gentleman were still about.

Ben did not descend himself. At least, not immediately. He waited for an explosion, the sound of which, he had little doubt, would reach him when it came; and he waited, to his surprise, with an unexpected calmness. He did not realise that his calmness was due to the very fact that the situation had got out of hand and that since it was now beyond him he no longer had to worry about making any decision. Temporarily he had ceased to be an actor in the drama of No. 19, Billiter Road. He had become the audience or, more correctly speaking, the listener.

He expected the explosion to occur at the bottom of the stairs, for after the crash which had concluded Mr Wavell's too rapid descent he had visualised the unhappy agent lying helplessly on the ground. No explosion took place. Instead, a sudden scuffling rose from the basement, obliterating the diminishing sound of Mrs Wavell's footsteps. The scuffling was followed by what seemed to be the swift closing of a door, which was itself followed by a muffled exclamation.

The exclamation did not come from Mrs Wavell. Creeping now to the top of the stairs, Ben saw her motionless figure standing at the bottom. She was staring along the passage, past the kitchen door, as though pausing to consider what next to do. All at once her back stiffened, and she began to move again, going along the passage till he lost sight of her. He heard her stop a second time, and then, after another pause, her voice broke the silence venomously.

'Come out! I know you're in there! Come out!'

There was no response. She called again, more loudly.

'Didn't you hear me? Come out—or am I to open it for you?'

She evidently did so, and now the exclamation came from herself. Sharp as a pistol shot, it reflected both astonishment and rage.

'So *that's* why you—!'

A rush of footsteps broke into her sentence. Someone appeared to have developed panic. An instant later Mr Wavell loomed meteorically at the foot of the stairs, began to mount with a curious lopsided motion, swerved round, and vanished again. Another door opened and closed with a bang. Then, silence once more.

Was this the moment to go down? Ben guessed that Mr Wavell had made his escape through the back door, but he had no solution of the cause of such an ignominious flight, nor of the silence that ensued after it. Why hadn't Mrs Wavell made any attempt to follow him? Or why, if she had decided to let him go, did she not return up the stairs?

Suddenly her voice sounded again. It was shrill with rage.

'Have you nothing to say for yourself?'

Who was she talking to?

'Trollop!'

Response came in the form of an hysterical gurgle, and Ben's heart missed a beat. Hesitating no longer, he clattered down the stairs, and came upon Mrs Wavell standing outside a cupboard, staring at someone still inside it. The inmate was the other, the far more attractive lady.

Mrs Wavell turned to Ben.

'I suppose *you* knew of this?' she challenged, icily.

'Knoo wot?' gulped Ben.

'How much have you been paid to keep their secret?'

Ben shook his head.

'Yer got it wrong, mum.'

'Oh, no! I've got it right!' She turned back to the cupboard. 'The next person you pick up to have an affair with, make sure first that he does not talk in his sleep. And you'd better start looking for him at once, for you won't be seeing any more of my husband, I assure you! No, don't try and explain. It will only be waste of time. I can find my own way out. Good-morning!'

She did not leave by her husband's route. They watched her march up the stairs and heard her bang the front door.

18

Oasis

'Nah, where are we?' asked Ben.

'Please!' she answered, dully. 'I need a minute to get over this!'

Her eyes were dazed. She had passed her moment of hysterics in the cupboard, and had now grown limp. Ben did not like the look of her.

''Ave a sit dahn,' he suggested.

The suggestion was somewhat pointless in the absence of a chair. She began to sway slightly, and he took hold of her arm.

'We'll go in the kitching,' he said.

She accepted his assistance mechanically, and when he had got her into the kitchen she fainted. The one fortunate thing in the unhappy situation was that the blackout occurred just as he was lowering her into a chair. He held her until he was sure she would not fall off, and then, placing another chair near her, sat down himself.

He never knew what to do with people who fainted. Corpses, yes. You just ran away from them. But faints?

146

You had to stand by to give 'em a hand when they came to. There was nothing to do while the faint was on, or if there was he'd never learned it. He wouldn't have minded a bit of a faint himself, because then life would have become a lovely blank into which all its problems would have vanished.

And, lummy, he was surrounded with problems! They weren't only in the kitchen. At least, not at the moment they weren't, but you never knew when some of them might come popping along! The two major problems outside the kitchen were Mr Black and that locked cellar. He'd have to get into the locked cellar somehow! But meanwhile he had to deal with the insensible problem in the kitchen chair.

'I don't expeck she's bin through not 'arf wot I bin through,' he reflected, as he watched her face for signs of recovery and noted its fatigue, 'but she's bin through somethink!'

Then an idea occurred to him. The obvious solution of every trouble in every English home. Tea! Of course, that was it! A nice cup of tea, ready and waiting for her the moment she opened her eyes. What happened if she didn't open her eyes? Lummy, *she* wasn't going to join the corpses, was she? He set aside the unpalatable thought, which was dissipated finally a few moments later just after he had got the kettle going. A small sigh whirled him round from the stove, and he saw that her eyes were open.

'Tike it easy,' he said.

She stared at him dully, and then suddenly sat up.

'Nah, jest you sit back agine fer a bit,' he advised. 'I don't want ter 'ear nothink from yer not till yer've 'ad a cup o' tea.'

She smiled faintly, and he turned back to the stove,

because there was gratitude in her smile, and Ben always felt orkward like when anybody was grateful to him.

''Ow yer feelin',' he asked the kettle, and then added, 'Oh! Don't answer, I fergot—yer ain't ter tork.'

Disobeying him, she replied, 'I'll soon be all right, and I've got to talk. I went off, didn't I?'

'No, yer stayed on,' said Ben.

'What?'

'The chair. See, yer come dahn on it jest right.'

'Please don't make me laugh.'

'Wot's funny? Corse, miss, yer marth's yer own, but I'd keep it fer that cup o' tea afore yer uses it fer torkin', honest I would.'

This time she obeyed him, closing her eyes again until the kettle had nearly boiled. He was just putting a finger in front of the spout, because with some kettles you can't see the steam even when the water's bubbling, but you can always feel it—he was just applying this test when she spoke again.

'I suppose that was Mrs Wavell?'

'Yer mean the one that's jest left?'

'Yes.'

'That's 'oo she sed she was.'

'What did she come for?'

'Well, it looked like Mr Wavell, didn't it?'

'Did you know he was still here?'

'*Oi!*'

'What's the matter?'

'Okay.' The steam had arrived. Sucking his finger, Ben said something unintelligible, and then started again. 'Kettle's boilin'. Doncher move. I'll bring yer yer cup in 'arf a mo'.'

148

When he brought it to her, she said, 'You know, you're a sort of an oasis.'

'Well, I bin called plenty,' he replied, 'but that's a new 'un!'

'What am I to call you? I can't remember if you've told me.'

'Ben's the nime.'

'Ben.'

'Am I ter know your'n, or ain't that the way yer wants it?'

She hesitated for a moment, then answered, 'I am Jennifer Bretherton.'

Bretherton. Lummy! Of course! . . .

'Go on!' he exclaimed.

'You didn't guess?'

'No, miss.' Now Ben was beginning to understand her interest. 'Yer mean—'is—'is wife?'

She shook her head.

'His sister.'

'Sister. Oh, I see. Leastwise, not orl of it.'

'You see why I want to find out all I can about the murder of my brother.'

'Yus, but not wot's brought yer 'ere. Or 'ave yer tole me, and 'ave I fergot? If yer wants the truth, miss, there's so much goin' on inside me 'ead that I couldn't tell yer wot's there and wot ain't. If yer git me?'

'Ben,' said Miss Bretherton, solemnly, 'I think heaven must have sent you here! Suppose it had been somebody else? But you and I can work together.'

'Yer right abart that,' he agreed, 'but I ain't so sure abart the other.'

'What other?'

''Eving. Any'ow, if it was 'Eving wot sent me 'ere, don't expeck me ter thank it!'

'I won't,' she smiled. 'I'll do the thanking. Aren't *you* going to have a cup? There looks enough in that pot for two.'

While they drank tea, and in the strange silence that seemed now to have settled on the house, Jennifer Bretherton told her story.

19

Exchange of Information

'I've told you, haven't I,' began Miss Bretherton, 'that I've worked for Mr Wavell. I was with him for about a year, and don't ask me why I stayed so long with the odious man! I started by disliking him, and ended by loathing him. In fact, when I left him it was because of his rotten behaviour.'

'Yer mean 'e wasn't honest like?' asked Ben.

'I am sure he wasn't honest like,' replied Miss Bretherton, 'but I didn't mean that. What I meant was—well, I can't say that I like Mrs Wavell much better from my one meeting with her, but I'm not surprised she goes chasing after him!'

'I git yer! 'E was too wot's called fresh?'

'He was. Slimey. Still I'm not going to talk any more about that. It's his dishonesty that concerns us most now, because it's through that—I think—yes, it must be—that you and I are here at this moment. Oh, dear! It's all such a tangle—I hardly know where to begin.'

'Did yer brother work fer 'im, too?' asked Ben.

'Oh, no. My brother was a private detective. Sort of. I

mean by that that sometimes he worked for other people—
was engaged for special jobs—but at other times he worked
for himself. On his own. He had—he had a passion for
puzzles. That kind of mind. When he'd solved them he
presented the solution to whoever it concerned. I'm not
explaining this very well.'

'I'm with yer so fur,' Ben assured her. "E was one o'
them curiosity blokes wot carn't see a knife on the floor
withaht thinkin', "'Oo done wot?"'

'That's a perfect description!'

'And was it 'im fahnd aht that Mr Wavell wer'n't honest?'

'I don't know how much he found out, but I do know
he was working on it up to—until yesterday.'

'Ah!'

'Why do you say that?'

'I was jest thinkin' that it sorter fitted.'

'What fitted?'

''Im workin' on it. See, when I see 'im on the seat, 'e 'ad
a note-book it looked like, and 'e was studyin' it so 'ard
'e didn't seem to be thinkin' o' nothink helse. I expeck that
was why 'e never noticed the bloke wot was be'ind 'im.'

She suppressed a little shudder.

'Very likely. Of course you don't know what happened
to the note-book?'

'Afraid not, miss.'

'The man who brought you here—who called himself
Smith—you don't know whether he had it on him?'

'No, miss. Was—was it that they was arter?'

'They must have wanted it, but of course it wasn't only
that. If they'd stolen the note-book, my brother could have
repeated what he'd written in it. He was killed because he
had too much knowledge.'

'Oh—yer think it was that?'

'I'm certain it was that.'

'Then, p'r'aps,' said Ben, looking at her solemnly, 'it'd be better fer you not ter 'ave too much knowledge?'

'You mean, safer?'

'Well, yus.'

'What about your knowledge?'

'Eh?'

'What are *you* doing here?'

'I git yer—on'y, see, I'm dif'rent.'

'Yes, you're different, Ben. It isn't your brother who's been murdered. So why don't you cut and run?'

Ben smiled rather whimsically.

'Yer fergettin', miss. It wouldn't be Ben runnin', it would be Marmerduke.' He explained. 'See, that's wot I calls me new fice. They've sorter fixed me 'ere, like I told yer, and I wanter git back on 'em!'

Miss Bretherton nodded.

'Then we won't worry any more about the risks,' she said. 'If our motives are different, our object is the same.'

'That's right. Ter git Smith on the end of a rope!'

'If he did it.'

'We needn't worry our 'eads abart that, miss. I seen 'im do it.'

'But there's something else we have to do as well. At least, I have. To finish my brother's work for him.'

'Well, I'm in on that, too,' answered Ben. ''Ow fur 'ad 'e got?'

'I wish I knew!'

'Yer ain't told me yet 'ow much yer do know. I expeck I can add a bit. Or wot started yer brother orf on it? But that's my fault, 'cos I keeps on interruptin'.'

'I don't mind your interruptions—they're rather helpful,' she said. 'How did my brother start? It was I who started him.'

''Ow was that?'

'I told you I left the firm because I disliked Mr Wavell, and that was true, but I didn't dislike him only because of his behaviour to me. I felt there was something crooked in his business dealings as well, although I couldn't put my finger on anything definite. Once when I was with my brother—we didn't live together, I have a small flat and he lived all over the place, wherever his jobs took him— once I mentioned my feelings to him, and he became interested. I was rather surprised at his interest.'

'P'r'aps 'e knew somethink already?' suggested Ben.

'He may have. I can't say.'

'Wot did yer 'ave ter tell 'im?'

'At first it was just my general feeling that came out of a few small incidents, and also Mr Wavell's rather furtive attitude. Then he—my brother—began asking questions, and drew out more than I'd realised there was to tell. For instance, I sometimes worked in his private office—too often towards the end!—but he always sent me out of the room on some thin pretext when a certain person telephoned.'

'Thin wot, miss?'

'Pretext. Excuse.'

'I git yer. 'E didn't want yer ter 'ear 'oo it was, eh?'

'But I always knew it was the same person, by the sudden change of his voice.'

'Not a lidy?'

'I didn't think so—but why don't *you*?'

''Cos my guess is it wer' Smith!'

She considered the suggestion, and suddenly asked,

'Didn't you tell me that Smith had a small brown moustache, or have I imagined it?'

''E 'as a small brahn mustache,' answered Ben, 'but I carn't remember if I tole yer.'

'Then it *may* have been Smith.'

''Ow's that? Yer carn't see a mustache over the telerphone!'

'Of course not, but—wait a minute!' She thought hard. 'I believe I've seen Smith!'

'That's right, yer saw 'im ahtside 'ere when yer left in a 'urry—'

'No, I don't mean then, and that was only for a few moments. I didn't recognise him. But somebody called at the office one day, and was with Mr Wavell for a long while in his private room. *He* had a small brown moustache, I'm almost sure. He never came again, as far as I know, but it was after his visit that Mr Wavell began to be so furtive and nervy, and I always felt that this man was the person who telephoned those times I was sent out of the room. Then, another thing,' she went on. 'I used to make out lists of houses for our clients, but presently Mr Wavell began making some out himself. He always gave these lists personally, and I got an idea he didn't want anybody else to see them—apart from the clients he gave them to. Once when I offered to type one for him—he'd mislaid the copy, and the client was waiting—he got quite snappy.'

'And that was one o' the things yer brother thort fishy, eh?'

'Yes. My brother was very interested in those private lists.'

'And you never saw any of 'em?'

'I hadn't seen any when I first spoke to my brother, but I had an opportunity about a week later. I went to Mr Wavell's private office with some letters, and he'd just been called away on some matter or other. I saw he'd been making out some lists, and they were on his desk.' She paused, then asked, 'What would *you* have done?'

'Wot you did,' answered Ben, with a wink.

She smiled. 'After all, why not? There they were, and I'd had no instructions that they were private. So I had a quick look at three of them, and when next I saw my brother I told him all I could remember. They were just ordinary lists of houses, but one or two things struck me. They mightn't have if I hadn't been suspicious and on the look-out for anything unusual. Only one of the addresses was repeated on all three forms, and it was always the fourth on the list—and it *wasn't* on our books. I don't suppose I have to tell you what the address was?'

'Nummer 19, Billiter Road,' said Ben.

'Yes. Does anything strike you?'

'Yus!'

'What?'

'The blokes 'e gives them lists ter was on'y interested in Nummer Nineteen, Billiter Road.'

'That was what my brother said.'

'Wot else did 'e say?'

'He said that this was just a method of giving them the address, and that of course they weren't bona fide clients.'

'Bony wot?'

'They weren't genuine clients—'

'Bogus! I git yer.'

'And he said that Mr Wavell was probably a go-between who was used to direct the bogus clients to this house.'

'Did 'e say why 'e thort Mr Wavell was this 'ere go-between?'

'He said there were two possible reasons—either he was being paid for it or was being blackmailed into it.'

'Yer mean, 'ooever was at the bottom of the bizziness knew somethink abart Mr Wavell that'd come aht if 'e didn't do wot 'e was told?'

'Yes.'

'Well, nah I've got another guess, miss.'

'What is it?'

'Might the person they'd tell, if 'e wasn't a good boy, be' is wife?'

Miss Bretherton regarded him with admiration.

'I think you've got it, Ben!' she exclaimed, 'and—'

''Arf a mo', miss,' interrupted Ben, in a lower tone, with a sudden glance towards the door. 'We'd better keep our voices dahn a bit more, p'r'aps.'

Reminded that they were in the middle of the situation they were discussing, Miss Bretherton accepted the advice.

'You're right, of course. Sorry. I was going to say—you know Mrs Wavell found me in that cupboard with Mr Wavell?'

'That's right.'

'Oh, dear, we're dodging all over the place, but I think I'll tell you about that now. After our last talk, when you had to go up to answer the bell—'

'And let in Mr Wavell and Mr Black—'

'Black? Who's he? No, never mind that yet! You thought I was going, but I didn't. I hid in the cupboard—I wasn't going to leave—and presently I heard Mr Wavell go by, talking to someone—oh, was *that* Mr Black?' Ben nodded. 'Then I thought Mr Wavell came back again, though he wasn't talking this time, and after that I kept opening the cupboard door and listening, waiting for him to go. I heard you talking to him upstairs, though I couldn't hear what you said. And then when he came hurrying down again I shut the cupboard door, and nearly died when he opened it and came flying in! So, I'm glad to say, did he!'

'Did 'e wot?'

'Nearly die! He bounced out again just before Mrs Wavell came along and found me. Do you wonder I had a black-out?' She made a helpless little gesture. 'I'm telling you this in the wrong place, but you had to hear what happened some time, and it does all lead back to this. Did Mrs Wavell think *I* was Mr Wavell's dark secret, and has that wretched demented man been babbling about it in his sleep? You heard what Mrs Wavell said to me about that!'

'I expeck that's the way of it,' agreed Ben, 'but it don't git us no nearer the dark secret o' this 'ouse! Did yer brother git on ter *that*?'

'I am quite sure he did—or very nearly,' answered Miss Bretherton, grimly, 'but he didn't tell me anything that he found out. In fact, he ordered me to drop the matter, and as I'd already given notice, that was easy.'

'But 'e didn't drop the matter,' said Ben.

'Unfortunately, no,' she replied. 'I wish to God he had! He must have come here at some time or other—'

'Yus,' interrupted Ben, 'and 'ad a 'eart-ter-'eart with the larst caretaiker!'

She looked startled. 'Didn't you say—?' She took from her pocket the unfinished note which Ben had swept off the top of the dresser. 'Of course—this would be from—?'

''Ave yer read it?' asked Ben.

'Yes.'

'Arter I left yer? While yer was waitin' dahn 'ere?'

'Yes.'

'Well, then, miss—wot do *you* think?'

'It was from the last caretaker.'

'To yer brother—'

'Yes. But he never got it.'

'That's right. If 'e 'ad got it, we wouldn't 'ave it. And 'e never got it, the way I works it aht, 'cos it was never finished, and it wer'n't finished 'cos the caretaiker was interrupted while 'e was writin' it, and when 'e 'eard some'un comin' while 'e was writin' it in this 'ere kitching 'e chucks it up or 'ides it on top o' the dresser, meanin' ter finish it laiter on. Yer might say the top o' the dresser was a funny plice ter choose, and if yer do, well, so do I, but it was up there, any'ow, so yer carn't argue it was anywhere else, if yer git me. P'r'aps 'e was standin' at the dresser writin' it, usin' it as a desk like, and when 'e 'ears the footsteps in the passidge 'e thinks "Gawd 'elp me," 'e would if 'e thort it was the monnertrocity, 'e'd git in a proper panic then, and 'e screws the paiper up and chucks it up, see, yer can see it's been screwed, and then—'

He paused, for a fresh breath, and also because what came next wasn't going to be very nice. But here they were, working it all out, and this wasn't the time to mince matters. Miss Bretherton made no comment during the pause. She was following Ben's lurid reconstruction intently, striving to keep her mind steady through its horror. The horror had been increased by her queer companion's reference to the 'monnertrocity.'

'We've got ter 'ave it,' muttered Ben.

'Yes—go on,' she replied.

'No good blinkin' facks, miss.'

'No, no! Go on! And then——?'

'And then the some'un comes in. Mind yer, it mightn't of bin the monnertrocity. It might of been Smith—or I wouldn't put it past Mr Wavell. I reckon 'e's ripe ter put 'iself in the way of the rope, if 'e's pushed to it. Any'ow, we don't know 'oo come. But we do know that, well something 'appened ter the caretaiker, and it could 'ave 'appened jest as well then as laiter, couldn't it?'

'Do you know what happened to him?' asked Miss Bretherton.

'Matter o' fack, miss, I do,' answered Ben.

'They—killed him?'

'Yus.'

'Is that a guess, or do you *know* it?'

'I knows it, miss.'

'How?'

'I seen 'im dead.'

'*What!*' she gasped.

'That's right. Last night, it was. See, there's a locked door at the end o' the passidge, and I 'ad a squint through the key'ole, and there was the caretaiker lyin' dead on the grahnd with some'un lookin dahn on 'im by the light of a torch.'

'I see. How frightful!' she murmured. 'But—Ben—how do you know it was the caretaker?'

'Oh, I got that orf of Smith nex' mornin'. That is, this mornin'. 'E kep' on sayin' wot 'appened to the larst caretaiker, so's I wouldn't go and do somethink wot'd mike 'em do the sime ter me. 'E took me in the cellar, Smith did, ter 'ave a look, but corse the corpse 'ad bin took away by then. Yus, but Sammy was lyin' there dead, instead—'

'Sammy?'

'Eh? Sammy was the cat. They killed 'im, too, blarst 'em! They ain't goin' ter git away with that!'

She gave him a curious glance.

'You seem more worried by the cat than the caretaker,' she said.

'Well—I mean ter say,' replied Ben. 'A cat! Wot wasn't doin' no 'arm ter nobody!'

'Is that door still locked?'

'Yus. Smith locked it agine arter we come aht.'

'Why did he take you in?'

'Why did 'e? I've fergot. Oh, no, I got it! It was arter wot I sed abart seem' the deader on the grahnd. See, it was this mornin' 'e took me in, and I was tellin' 'im abart wot I seen the night afore.'

'Yes, can we go back to that for a moment? You said you saw someone looking at—at the dead man?'

'That's right, miss.'

'Then you know who *that* was?'

'Ah, I couldn't see 'im extinct. See, yer carn't see 'oo's 'oldin' the torch, not in the dark. But it wer'n't Smith, and—no, it wer'n't Wavell, so wot I work aht is that it wer' the stacher—leastwise, that's wot I called it afore I thort it must of bin the monnertrocity. 'Ave I tole yer abart 'im? There's somethink wrong with 'is feet, 'cos when 'e walks abart in the night, like wot 'e did, 'e don't go pat-pat or thump-thump, but woosh-woosh. Yus, and ter go back a bit further still, ter wot we was torkin' abart afore we went orf the track like, it was proberly 'im wot killed the caretaker so's the caretaker wouldn't 'ave no more meetin's with yer brother, see, they must of got on ter it, p'r'aps they mide the caretaker talk a bit afore they finished 'im orf, and then, arter a bit of a confab, mindyer, this is on'y guessin' agine, but it looks like it, don't it, one of 'em, it bein' Smith, goes aht arter yer brother, and gits 'im, too.' Ben stopped and blinked.

''Ow do we go, miss? Is that the lot, or 'ave we missed anythink aht?'

Miss Bretherton passed a hand across her spinning forehead.

'I think I've told you all my side of it,' she answered, 'though I wouldn't be sure. My mind's a bit numb. But there's something you still have to tell me.'

'Wozzat?' Ben enquired.

'About Mr Black.'

'Oh, yus. Mr Black,' repeated Ben, and removing his eyes from Miss Bretherton's, he gazed uncomfortably at the kitchen door.

'Tell me,' she said.

'Well—see—I 'ardly know abart Mr Black meself yet,' he parried.

'But what do you know?'

'On'y that 'e come at ten-thirty with Mr Wavell, and was s'posed ter be lookin' over the 'ouse.'

'Well? Did he do it?'

'Look over the 'ouse?'

'Yes, of course!'

'I showed 'im one room, and then Mr Wavell took 'im dahn 'ere ter the bisement.'

She nodded. 'That was when I was in the cupboard, and heard them go by. You didn't come down with them?'

'No.'

'Why not?'

'Mr Wavell didn't want me. 'E tole me ter stay above, ready like, in caise I was wanted.'

'I see. And you weren't wanted?'

'No.'

'Did you see Mr Black again?'

'No.'

'And when Mr Wavell returned by the cupboard, he wasn't talking to anybody, so he probably returned alone.'

'Yer'd think it.'

Her mind harped back. Suddenly she shot another question. It was one Ben had been waiting for.

'Didn't you mention something you had to give to Mr Wavell when he came?'

'That's right, miss,' answered Ben. 'A parcel. 'E arsked fer it, and 'e went aht o' the room I was showin' Mr Black over ter open it—leastwise, that's wot it must of bin. And then they went dahn tergether, and on'y 'im come up agine. And then 'is old woman come along, and I reckon yer knows wot 'appened arter that!'

'Yes, I know!' she returned, grimly. 'I wouldn't be in Mr Wavell's shoes at this moment!'

'Yer right,' agreed Ben, 'though that don't mean I mightn't be ready ter chainge with 'im! Well, there we are, miss, and it seems ter me that p'r'aps we ought ter stop torkin' nah, and ter start doin'!'

'I agree,' responded Miss Bretherton. 'Only—doing *what*?'

Ben hesitated. ''Ave *you* any idea?'

Rather to his surprise, she nodded. 'I think it's the same idea as your own,' she said. 'We've got to get through that locked door into the cellar!'

20

The Enemy Closes In

Miss Bretherton's guess was only partly correct. It had been Ben's idea to have another shot at the cellar, but an alternative idea was taking its place. It was not a new idea, and it was an obvious idea, but equally obvious had been Ben's reasons hitherto against adopting it. Now, however, he had Miss Bretherton to think of as well as himself.

'Yus, some'un's gotter git inter that there cellar,' he replied, 'and that's a fack, but 'ow abart letting the pleece do it?'

She regarded him solemnly.

'I thought you didn't want the police here just yet,' she said.

'Well, it may put me on a spot,' he answered, 'but there's others ter think abart, ain't there?'

'Do you mean Mr Black?'

'Well, 'e's one of 'em.'

'Who else?'

'Wot abart you?'

'Me—?'

164

'Yus, miss. It ain't goin' ter be no birthday party messin' arahnd that there cellar.'

'I didn't come here expecting a birthday party,' she returned. 'I came here—'

She paused, almost as though wondering herself, while Ben regarded her uneasily.

'Yus, yer come 'ere, and yer'd better not of,' he said. 'Yer orter've kep' aht of it, like yer brother sed.'

'But that was before—all this happened,' she reminded him. 'Would he have expected me to sit still now and do nothing?'

'Well, no,' agreed Ben. 'Wot 'e'd of expected yer to do would be ter go ter the pleece.' And then he suddenly asked, 'Yus, why didn't yer?'

She frowned.

'The police came to me,' she answered.

'Yus—corse, they would! So why—?'

'Didn't I tell them about this house? This may surprise you. It wasn't till after they had gone that I thought about this house.'

That did surprise Ben.

'Go on!' he exclaimed.

'It's true I might have thought of it,' she said, 'but it's also true that I didn't. Remember I wasn't working on this with him. I just started him off, and then he went on with it by himself. He didn't talk to me about it—I hadn't even seen him for a month. No,' she went on, in self-extenuation, 'there was no special reason why I should have connected this house with his death. He had other enemies—like most others engaged in his kind of work.'

'I git yer,' nodded Ben. 'But wot abart when yer *did* think of it?'

'When I did think of it, I came right here.'

'Withaht goin' ter the pleece fust?'

'What should I have told them? There was nothing really definite. Anyway, whether I was right or wrong I followed my impulse and came along myself to see whether there was anything to find out here. I hadn't much hope, you may like to know, when you opened the door to me. Of course,' she added, thoughtfully, 'I could have gone to the police when I left you last night. That side-whisker of yours was certainly suspicious! But there still wasn't anything really definite to report to them, and I decided that we must finish our interrupted conversation, you and I, before I brought the police in.'

'Yus, yer said yer was comin' back,' answered Ben, 'but nah we 'ave finished our conversashun—'

'Which, among other things, has shown me why *you* haven't been for the police,' she interrupted, 'and why you didn't want them!'

'A fat charnce I 'ad ter git 'em if I '*ad* wanted 'em! Yus, but nah it's dif'rent, miss,' he went on. 'Not on'y you gotter be kep' aht of it—I mean, see, if there's ter be any rough stuff, git me?—but there's this Mr Black. See, them others was dead afore I could do nothink abart 'em, and when yer dead yer dead, but, well, we dunno yet wot's 'appened ter Mr Black, and if 'e's in that cellar wantin' 'elp, we gotter see it's the kind of 'elp 'e needs! That's right, ain't it?'

'Yes, it's right,' Miss Bretherton replied, 'all but one thing.'

'Wozzat?'

'You don't *really* think, do you, that I'm going home to knit while what you call the rough stuff is going on?'

'We wouldn't want yer 'ere, miss.'

She smiled at him. 'Don't be too sure of that! After the rough stuff come the bandages! Never mind, leave that for the moment,' she exclaimed, anticipating more protests. 'We're agreed that the police must be fetched, and we can decide later how we sort ourselves out. Who'll go? I expect I'd better.'

'Yus, they're more likely ter believe you.'

'One thing I'm going to make them believe is that *you're* straight. What will you do while I'm gone?'

'Eh? Oh—well, I dessay I'll mike a start like.'

'No!' she said, sharply. 'You must wait!'

'Not if the pleece keeps yer torkin'.'

'They won't! I'll see they don't! Wait till I come back with them—don't forget, somebody's got to be here to let us in, and we don't want to be let in by the wrong person! It might be your monstrosity, whoever that is,' she added, grimly. 'I'll slip out the back way.'

She jumped up from her chair, then paused a little uncertainly now the moment for action had arrived.

'Nothing more, is there—before I go?'

'No, miss,' replied Ben, 'barrin' makin' sure the bobby yer bring back is a good strong 'un!'

'I'll bring back a whole army of strong ones, if I can,' she promised, now making for the door. 'Well, I'm away. Look after yourself.'

He followed her to the back door, and after she had slipped out he waited a few seconds, closed the door, and then turned towards the passage that led to the locked cellar. Wait? No bloomin' fear! There'd been a durn sight too much waiting already, and he realised with something of a shock, and also an uneasy sense of shame, how long had elapsed since Mr Black had vanished. But was it his

167

fault? One thing had happened on top of another, and he couldn't recall that he'd had a moment. After Mr Black had gone down, Mr Wavell had come up, and then there'd been Mrs Wavell, and then there'd been Miss Bretherton's black-out, and then there'd been that long talk which had had to be got through—or had it? He might change his opinion if, after he had broken into the cellar, never mind how he was going to do it, he found Mr Black hanging from the ceiling on a rope!

He wished he hadn't thought of that. Ben did not need to paint pictures, he often told himself. It would be a waste of time. They came into his mind with an unwelcome vividness, and against that dim mental background they showed up more clearly, and also more startlingly, than in any frame! The picture in Ben's mind now was of Mr Black at the end of the rope upside down.

All this jumble of vision and thought happened on the way to the cellar door. Now he was at the door, and his hand was moving cautiously towards the handle. But he drew it back before it got there, and decided to apply his eye to the keyhole first. About to stoop, he suddenly stiffened. Someone was moving in the passage behind him.

The late vision of Mr Black hanging upside down was replaced by a far worse one. It was of a huge ape-like man with two heads and four spongy feet. It was really time, perhaps, for Ben to meet the monnertrocity face to face—or, in his present conception, face to two faces—for its shape and aspect were becoming so increasingly horrific that nothing short of the reality could wipe it out!

He tried to move. He found that he couldn't. Somehow he'd got stuck. 'I know wot it is,' he decided. 'I'm dead. See, it's orl 'appened, but when yer dead yer fergit it. See, it's orl over, and yer in the nex' plice, wherever that is. Corse, that's it. I'm dead.'

A moment later, or a fraction of a moment, for you can die and be born again in a fraction, he made the disastrous discovery that he was not dead. He could still hear the sound, and it was coming closer . . . Oh, well, never mind. He soon would be. And that was what he wanted. wasn't it?

He tried to think of something nice. The little girl he had helped across the road came into his mind. He thought of her hard. We never know how we help each other . . .

'What are you doing?'

The words fell upon his ear almost in a whisper. He found now that he could move. He turned round to face, not the monnertrocity, but Miss Bretherton.

''Arf a mo',' he said. 'I'm goin' ter be sick.'

But he just saved himself, and found himself listening to her explanation.

'It's no good. They're outside,' she said.

''Oo?' gulped Ben.

'Two men. One is Smith, the other I don't know, but they were standing, talking. Luckily I saw them before they saw me. What were you doing?'

'Eh? I—I jest thort I'd 'ave a squint through the key'ole.'

'You looked as if something had happened.

'You 'appened! Are yer sure it was Smith?'

'Yes, quite sure. From your description, and my recollection. I've no idea who the other man is—'

'I 'ave, miss. It's proberly the bloke that was with 'im when I was brort 'ere and 'oo pertended ter be that bobby. Was they comin' in?'

'Just talking, and glancing towards this house. They were across the road. They may be here any moment.'

''Ow abart boltin' the back door?'

'I've done it! Is the front door bolted?'

'I dunno. No, I don't think it is, but Smith sed 'e could git in if it was. Any'ow I better go up and 'ave a look.'

'Will that do any good?'

'Yer mean, are we goin' ter try and keep 'em aht?'

'Yes, that's what I mean. We've got to plan something or other, haven't we?'

'That's right, miss, and I reckon the fust plan is ter find aht if they're comin' or goin'. P'r'aps they're jest goin' on standin' there. Watchin' like.'

'Suppose they are?'

'Yer mean, withaht no charnce of slippin' by 'em ter fetch the pleece?'

'Yes.'

Ben thought. 'Well, miss, they'd see yer, but they'd 'ardly go fer yer. In 'ere, they might, but not in the street.'

'I agree to that, but if they saw me, what *would* they do?'

''Ow's this fer a guess? One'd foller yer, t'other'd come in 'ere ter see wot was up.'

'And then? Forget me for a moment, and the one who would be following me—I expect I'd find my policeman just the same and bring him along. But what about you?' She shook her head. 'I'd have given them the signal, and the man who came in here would act upon it, and this is *my* guess! When I arrived here with my policeman you'd be missing!'

Ben retorted, 'Yus, and if we both stays 'ere we'll both be missin'! Nah listen, miss, I'm goin' ter tork sense! Like

yer brother would. Yer ain't goin' ter stay 'ere, and I dunno
wot's up with me fer lettin' yer stay so long, that's a fack.
Mr Black'll 'ave ter waite till I git yer aht, and I'm goin'
up nah ter the front door fer a look-see—yer know, careful
like—and I'm arskin' yer ter stay where yer are, or, no, in
the kitching, till I comes dahn. If they've gorn, then you
'op it, and if they 'aven't—well, then I got another way I
think I can beat 'em.'

'What's your other way?'

'I think they calls it creetin' a disversion, or somethink
like that. Say yer chucks a bottle aht of a winder ter make
'em look that way, then while they're lookin' that way you
pops orf the other. Any'ow, that's if they ain't gorn, and
I'm goin' up nah ter find aht.'

Before she could offer any further protest he slid by her
and made for the stairs.

He could not believe as he mounted them that the last
time he had done so was to answer Mr Wavell's ring at
10.30. He had no idea of the present time, for he did not
run to a wrist-watch, but by now 10.30 seemed many
hours ago. He prayed as he mounted that either Miss
Bretherton had been mistaken, or that the two men had
merely paused by the house and had now passed on. He
had spoken confidently about his alternative plan, but his
voice had contained more confidence than he felt. The only
thing he was sure of was that Miss Bretherton had now
become his first concern, and that somehow or other he
must get her away from this danger zone. See, she must
of been through a bit, losin' her brother like that, and then
she was a nice lidy, too, yer couldn't get away from it.

Reaching the front door, he wondered how he was
going to get a squint without being squinted at himself.

To open the door would be folly. The fanlight was too high to reach. What about the letter-box? But it proved one of those inconvenient ones, with a metal flap over the slit that only lifted a little distance. Possibly if you got a stool and stood on it on your head you could see through a bit, but the bit you saw would be upwards, and a view of a chimney would be hardly worth the trouble.

''Ow abart a 'igher floor?' he wondered.

Yes, that was the wheeze. Go up to the next floor and see what was doing from a front room window. He ascended the flight on the lowest steps of which he had spent most of the night—was that why Sammy suddenly shot into his mind, and he looked down at his feet as though the cat might still be there?—and when he reached it, went into a front room. He crawled across the floor till he got to the window, and then cautiously raised his head till his eyes drew level with the glass.

'Gorn!' he sighed, with relief. Then he groaned. 'No, they 'aven't! There they are! Lummy, and nah they're crossin' the road!'

He twisted round, sped back to the door, and legged it down two flights in record time, reaching the bottom in a flat sprawl. As he picked himself up, feeling a little reproachful that Miss Bretherton did not appear to assist in the process, he called hoarsely,

'Oi! They're comin'!'

There was no reply. All at once the silence chilled him.

'Oi!' he called again. 'Oi, miss! Where are yer?'

On his feet once more, he began looking around. His heart thumped now with more than the physical exertion of speeding down stairs. He looked in the kitchen and the larder and the scullery and the cupboards. There was not a sign of her.

Then hope revived. Corse! She must of got a charnce while he was upstairs and took it. She was orf fer the pleece!

But the hope was dashed by a glance at the back door. It was still bolted.

21

The Locked Door

Ben's first impulse, in face of this proof that Miss Bretherton had vanished somewhere inside the house, was to unbolt the back door, rush out into the street, and yell, ''Elp!' In the emotion of the moment he did make a movement towards doing so. But then he realised that while he was rushing out through the back door, Smith and his companion would be coming in through the front door, and that when he returned with whoever had responded to his summons, both doors would probably be bolted again and Gawd knows what would be 'appenin' be'ind 'em! The situation outlined by Miss Bretherton herself had been substantially reversed; instead of her returning with help to find Ben missing, he would return through having found her missing!

And then what would he say to any passer-by who paused to enquire what was the matter? There might not be any passer-by, for Billiter Road was an unfrequented thoroughfare, and he might have to go into another to find them. He listened to his feverish voice trying to explain: 'Oi, there's a lidy in Nummer Nineteen wot's vanished, leastwise she seems ter of, it's ter do with that murder, the one yesterday—' (only yesterday) '—on the park seat, the one there's a pickchure of in terday's paipers, on'y corse it wasn't me wot done it but I knows 'oo did, and 'e's in there along with some others, and we gotter find 'er, lummy, 'urry up, wotcher waitin' for?' How long would it take, Ben wondered, to convince whoever heard such an oration that he wasn't, at best, a lunatic?

Once he had rushed out of another house—the number that time had been seventeen—and it had taken more than a bit to convince the fellow he had bounced into that he wasn't looney.

So, instead of acting on his first impulse, Ben turned from the back door and made for the cellar. He had not worked out any theory—he was afraid to—but everything bad seemed to have its origin behind that locked door, and so he obviously turned to it. 'Wot I gotter do,' he thought, deciding on the apparently impossible, 'is ter git that door open afore Smith and 'is pal come along. I gotter do it, see, I gotter do it—*some'ow*!'

He seized the handle violently, gave it a vicious twist, and shoved. It was wasted energy. The door swung inwards without any protest, and he entered the cellar in a swift slide along the cold floor.

22

Beyond the Cellar

Ben's entry into the cellar had been effected with such astonishing ease that for a moment all emotions saving that of surprise departed from him. He had sworn to achieve the impossible, and here he was actually doing it! But the miracle had to be credited to a kindly God rather than to Ben's own ingenuity. Kindly? Well, that seemed less certain in the sequel; but here he was, inside the locked cellar, after having done no more than turn the handle and push!

"Ow did it 'appen?' he wondered, as he slid across the floor till he came to a halt in the middle.

The obvious answer came to him the moment his brain began to function again. It had happened because the door had not been locked, and when the door of a room is not locked all you have to do to enter is to give the handle a twist. But the answer to the first question merely raised others. Why had not the door been locked? How long had it been unlocked? And where now were those who were believed to have been in the cellar? These, in Ben's conception, included Miss Bretherton, Mr Black, and the monnertrocity. Where had they gone?

Come to that, his dizzy mind went on (for although it was now functioning once more, it was still dizzy), you might add a couple to the crowd and ask where the dead caretaker and the dead cat had gone? Their spirits had departed permanently, but their bodies must have remained behind somewhere.

And now came an answer, which also appeared obvious, to that. Ben was still sitting on the ground at the spot where his momentum had been spent, and he was facing the opposite wall. It was the wall which contained the second, lower door in the cellar. Assumedly, the door of a cupboard. Assumedly, a very roomy cupboard. Assumedly, locked. Assumedly but not necessarily, after Ben's experience with the door from the passage.

Well, this second door had to be opened next, however terrifying what lay on the other side of it. And it had to be opened quickly, before the opportunity was taken from him. Vague sounds, coming from either the hall or the basement stairs, warned him that the opportunity would last for only a few more seconds, and leaping suddenly to his feet he ran back to the door to the passage. Was the key in the lock? Thank Gawd, it was! He turned it swiftly. This would give him a bit longer, for although he knew Smith had another key, he would have to work this key out of the lock before he could use his own.

How in any case Ben was going to rescue Miss Bretherton if he found her in the cupboard, whether Smith and his companion got into the cellar or remained outside, was beyond his knowledge. He had gained a short breather, and sufficient for the moment was the infinitesimal good thereof.

Momentarily secure from attack behind, he went to the cupboard. Pity it was so low. This meant that, when he had got the door open, he would have to duck to enter it, which would put him at a disadvantage with any foe. You can't hit while you duck. The thing to do therefore would be to open the door and then step aside, wouldn't it? And then if anythink came aht that you didn't like—*wang!*

There was a keyhole in the door. He put his ear to it. He heard nothing, but his ear was tickled by a cold draught. Next he tried his eye, with a similar result. He saw nothing, and his eye became instantly cold, as though a thin icy finger had been poked into it. All right. That was that—or them! Now for the acid test!

Straightening himself, he took hold of the knob and gently turned it. Exercising more caution now, he did not this time subject the handle to any violence but softly and gingerly gave it a little pull. Crikey! This door wasn't locked, either, and as it began to come towards him he quickly halted its movement. Then, after taking a deep breath, he pulled the door wide and sprang aside, his fists at the ready.

Nothing came out at him. He waited till he heard footsteps coming along the basement passage, took another deep breath, and moved to the doorway.

He peered into blackness. It was not the blackness of an ordinary cupboard; you can see hooks and shelves in that sort of blackness. It was the blackness of a tunnel, in which you can't see anything. In fact, it was not a cupboard. It was a passage.

Taking another deep breath, he entered the large black yawning mouth, and a moment after he had done so he became conscious of a queer change. Something seemed to have happened, but he had no idea what, and the first sign of the change was an abrupt blotting out of the sound of the footsteps outside the cellar. In spite of the urgency of his situation he jerked his head round, which brought him to the second sign; for gone, too, was the dim light of the cellar. Blackness now lay in his rear as well as ahead.

The door had swung to behind him.

'Gawd!' he gasped. ''Oo done that?'

He hoped the door itself had done it. Doors does close orl by theirselves sometimes, lummy, doesn't they? But however this door had closed, whether by some peculiarity of its own or by less appealing human agency, it settled things. There was no more time for deep breaths.

During the moments that followed Ben would have given a year of his life (if he had it to give, which seemed unlikely) for an electric torch. He had not even a match, and as he groped his way forward an old tune began to run round his mind. It ran round teasingly for several seconds before it dawned on him what the tune was. It was the tune of '"Will you walk into my parlour?" said the spider to the fly.' This wasn't the first time by a long chalk that Ben had been the fly, but he wished he could once be the spider, for a change!

At first as he groped through the darkness his weaving hands met nothing but space, but soon his left hand contacted a wall, and the wall was so close that he abruptly veered off his course a little to the right. This brought his other hand against hard brick, and the sudden transition from width to narrowness gave him a suffocating feeling. The walls seemed to have advanced on him from either side with the intention of squeezing him flat. Happily they did not advance any farther, remaining separated by barely

179

the width of his body, but the floor now began to give him concern, starting to slope away from beneath his feet, which he often put down without finding bottom. 'Am I goin' dahn ter 'Ell?' he wondered. The next instant it seemed like it. The gradient increased abruptly, he tripped, and wherever he was going down to, he went down head first.

The final stage of his journey was short but violently uncomfortable. He did not slide, he bumped, from which he gathered, while still in a condition to gather anything, that he was descending steps. Not soft, carpeted, cushiony steps, but hard unyielding steps, which hit him violently at every contact. He knew nothing of his arrival at the bottom. When consciousness returned he was lying face down on the ground, aching in every part of him, and with an odd disturbing sense of unnatural light somewhere round about.

Why did the light seem unnatural? He had no idea. Nor had he any idea why, in spite of its unnaturalness, there was something familiar about it, bringing back a memory without the usual accompaniment of what the memory was of. Light. A light. He dwelt vacuously on the word. He knew that round the corner of his memory there was considerably more to dwell on, but all he was fit for just now was something simple, and what could be simpler than a monosyllable? So he went on dwelling on the word light; but soon he added the longer word, artificial. Well, of course it would be artificial light. It had to be, didn't it, if he wasn't out in the open? All right, then. He was lying on the floor, and the floor was artificially lit.

Or—was it?

Opening one eye a little wider, he squinted sideways into

darkness. Where had the light gone? Had it ever been? 'It wer'n't no light,' he decided. 'It was jest stars. Yer gits 'em arter fallin' dahn stairs, doncher?' Falling down stairs. Yes, of course, he'd fallen down stairs, and the light he'd seen was jest the light yer sees arter the bump. That would explain why it had seemed both unnatural and familiar. Familiar because Ben had had countless bumps in his uncomfortable life, and unnatural because he had never really got used to them. So now the light was explained—he wouldn't see that again—but not the stairs. Where had he fallen from? . . .

Then he did see the light again. It was moving about him. And something—or somebody—was touching him. And now recollection came flooding back, developing that first unresolved memory on his return to consciousness. it was of the monnertrocity bending over the dead caretaker with an electric torch. And now was the monnertrocity bending over another caretaker with the torch? The other caretaker was Ben, though by a miracle not yet dead.

A voice which now sounded above him, however, seemed uncertain on the point.

'Is he finished?' asked the voice.

Ben recognised it. It was Smith's.

'Looks like it,' came another. Would this be Smith's companion? Whoever it was, Ben decided to go on looking like it. 'A crash down these stairs ought to crack anybody's skull!'

'You've said it—though we're talking about a thick one. He may be just unconscious.'

'Let's turn him over.'

'No, not yet. If he's dead he's dead, and if he isn't we don't want him butting in for a bit.'

'Do I get that?'

'What's the precise position here, constable?'

Constable? Was this a bobby!

'Now then, now then, I had quite enough of that last night!'

Of course! The bogus one! That proved the second speaker to be Smith's pal. Ben recognised the voice now, though it lacked the slow heaviness it had assumed in the role of policeman.

'I asked you what the position was, George?' repeated Smith.

Smith's pal—bogus bobby—George. All one. We're learnin'!

'How do *I* know the position,' George retorted.

'Exactly! You don't know it, and I don't know it, and Monkey-face can't tell it!'

Monkey-face?

'And so *now* perhaps you've got it?'

'You mean,' said George, 'we'd like to know more before we see the Chief?'

'That,' replied Smith, 'is what I mean. I want to know what happened here? Wavell was supposed to ring me up, but he didn't. Why didn't he? I tried the office, but he hadn't got back.'

'Quick work, if he had.'

'Yes, I dare say, if there was any hitch, but he shouldn't have been here more than five minutes, and anyhow he was supposed to phone me immediately he left, from the corner. And this fellow—how did *he* get in here. Was that *your* doing, Monkey-face?'

An incoherent gurgle, like a dumb man trying to speak, sent Ben's heart down into his boots. Was Monkey-face the monnertrocity?

'I've an idea, George,' Smith's voice went on, 'that if there's been any trouble, Monkey-face here may have had more than a little to do with it. He's been running around loose, you know. Is that the Chief's idea, or his?'

'I don't mind telling you,' replied George, 'that Monkey-face gives me the creeps! I can never get used to the knowledge that he can't hear what we're saying—and couldn't reply if he did!'

'He was wandering around last night.'

'Was he?'

'And he killed a cat.'

'What did he do that for?'

'Yes, what did you do it for, sweetheart? Case of one murder leads to another? Where I differ from you, Monkey-face, is that after I've had a go I like a bit of a rest, but once *you* start you can't stop! Was that cat the last thing you got rid of, or have you had some more fun this morning? If this chap on the floor you're eyeing so juicily *isn't* dead, you'll probably be given him as a final titbit—'

'Yes, and if he isn't dead,' interrupted George, nervily, 'he may be hearing all we're saying! Suppose he is?'

Smith gave a short laugh.

'Well, Georgie, suppose he is?'

'That's what I said.'

'I heard you. But go on with it. Suppose he is hearing all we say. Don't you trust him?'

'Do *you*?'

'I did the time I last left him . . . No, don't go, Monkey-face. If the Chief doesn't come along, we'll all beard him in his den together . . . *That's* right! . . . Where was I? I trusted him the time I last left him, but I want to know

what happened when Wavell and Black called to confirm
it, and if we find he *isn't* straight—so to put it—well, how
do you suppose he is going to get away from this tomb
with any knowledge we don't want broadcast, once he's
got down here? He knows a packet, anyway, and whether
he's for us or against us I don't imagine that the Chief
intends him to stay in the land of the living once the present
business is over.'

'What beats me,' said George, 'is why he was ever brought
into it.'

'And what beats me, Constable George,' retorted Smith,
'is how the Chief and I have ever kept *you* on the staff!
It hasn't been for your brain-power—I suppose it's just
because you're strong and obedient and willing, and know
which side your bread's buttered! You wonder why our
friend Jones was brought into it? He wasn't brought into
it—he was already in it, on that park seat! I wasn't going
to knife the two of them. Besides, George, unlike you and
Monkey-face, and even the Chief, I'm an artist. *You* would
be ready to paint the same picture over and over again if
it brought you in enough dough. I like variety—new
methods—new technique. I travel, like the White Knight,
equipped for all emergencies, and I fit my method to the
moment. You may not believe it, but I enjoy our friend
Jones, I delight in every second with him, and I divined
this would be so when I first clapped eyes on him. Risk?
Certainly. All true artists take risks, and I took the risk of
the photograph. After all,' added Smith, with amused irony,
'we *did* need a new caretaker. But don't get any wrong
ideas about me. I may shed a private tear when Jones is
put away, if his tumble hasn't put him away already, but
I won't interfere. Monkey-face shall have him.'

After a moment's silence, George exclaimed, sarcastically, 'You *don't* mean to say you've finished?'

'I believe I have,' answered Smith, 'although I could go on talking about Jones for ever. Come along. I hope we find the Chief in a good mood. I suppose one of us ought to stay behind with Jones, in case he comes to. Is Monkey-face to be trusted? In his present somewhat homicidal humour . . . Hallo! What was that?'

'I didn't hear anything.'

'I thought I did—and so did Monkey-face, by his succulent expression. It sounded like a woman's cry.'

23

Who's the Lady?

The three men standing above Ben nearly got the shock of their lives, for on hearing Smith's last words the alleged corpse only saved itself from leaping into the air by a superhuman effort. If Smith's ears had not deceived him and if he had truly heard a woman's cry, there could be no doubt in Ben's mind who the woman was.

Fortunately the superhuman effort was successful, and Ben's flattened form maintained its semblance of decease. He hoped that a little later he would deliver a surprise that would be a knock-out for the enemy, but if he delivered it now, the knock-out would be for himself and there would be no hope at all of saving Miss Bretherton. Therefore the surprise had to be postponed.

After a short pause, the interrupted conversation was resumed.

'It couldn't have been,' came George's voice.

'Why not?' replied Smith.

'What woman would it be? If Black's got a wife, he'd hardly have brought her with him!'

'He has got a wife, but she's on the other side of the Iron Curtain.'

'Oh! Is she?'

'Didn't you know?'

'How can I know what I'm not told?' retorted George, a note of sudden complaint in his tone.

'True,' admitted Smith sneeringly. 'And of course you could *never* guess!'

'Look here, I've had enough of your sarcasm! Give me any more and you'll learn something *you* never guessed! Suppose, for a change—what's the matter!'

'Monkey-face! Hold him!'

'Hey!'

'Blast! He's gone!'

Following the sound of a momentary scuffle, Ben heard once more the unpleasant spongy footsteps of the monner-trocity. As they faded away Smith swore, but his companion clearly had a different view of the departure.

'Good riddance!' said George. 'Let him go! Maybe the Chief can use him, and anyhow we don't want him here! We're talking a bit freely, and have you ever thought the fellow may be shamming?'

'I never waste time,' returned Smith, 'by thinking of impossible things.'

'Bah! Nothing's impossible down this hole! It's not even impossible that the Chief doesn't trust you and me, and that he uses Monkey-face as a private informer as well as a private executioner! Where the devil is he, and what's he up to at this moment?'

'He doesn't usually come out to meet us.'

'I know that. We have to go to him. And one time we may go to him and never come back—I've seen

Monkey-face looking at me sometimes as if he was just waiting for the word go!'

'George.'

'Yeah? What are you smiling at? If you've got anything to say, shoot!'

'I love you when you get all American. It sort of makes you feel tougher than you are, doesn't it?'

'Oh, shut up—!'

'Do you earn good money?'

'So do you.'

'Weren't you rather worse than penniless when I introduced you here, and incidentally weren't you also due for another little term of board and lodging at the Country's expense? You can't have your cake and eat it, George—and you can't earn good money in our profession without risk. That's why the money's good.'

George growled.

'All right! Leave that, and let's get back. There's no harm in minimising the risk, is there? What's this about the Iron Curtain? And Black's wife?'

'I've told you this is a big thing—'

'Yes, and that's all you've told me! "You're on duty to assist me in something big and bloody," you told me yesterday, and I'll say it was bloody! If it's as big, okay! Spill a bit more!'

'Here's a bit more,' answered Smith. 'A bit about Black's wife.'

'Yes, what about her?' asked George.

'She won't come to any harm on the other side of the Curtain so long as Black does what's wanted.'

'I see. And he came here to do it today?'

'Clever fellow!'

'What was it?'

'Perhaps I don't know.'

'And perhaps you do!'

'I may have an inkling, but what makes you think I'm the Chief's confidant? If you think I sit beside the Chief on his perch while he whispers all his secrets into my ear, you're wrong! Wait till I've got a perch of my own before you start pumping me. And that may not be so very long ahead, either. In fact, George—'

He broke off.

'Go on!' exclaimed George. 'In fact what?'

'Shall I tell you?'

'You know you're going to, so why waste time?'

'All right, here goes! Once we've cleared our present little pile I may be breaking away. The Chief rather cramps my particular style. He doesn't appreciate originality. Also this joint is getting a bit too hot . . . I say, George, is our corpse moving?'

The speaker would have been surprised had he realised that the corpse was wondering the same thing, for owing to a sudden and growing tickle on his nose he was discovering it almost impossible to maintain his motionless pose. Perspiration dripped from his forehead to moisten the floor against which it was pressed. Ben could stand much, having long learned the necessity of doing so, but the one thing he could not stand was a tickle on his nose. Upon his superhuman self-control during the next few seconds depended his very life. And added to the tickle on his nose now came the new burden of breath on the back of his neck. He didn't care much for that, either, because it meant that somebody was bending over him for a closer scrutiny—Smith or George, but not, thank Gawd, the monnertrocity! After a short agonising period, the breath left his neck, while the tickle remained on his nose.

'Well?' came George's voice.

'If he isn't dead as a doornail,' replied Smith, 'he's got such a black-out that he wouldn't need any anaesthetic for an operation. What was I saying?'

'You were talking about clearing off.'

'Ah, so I was. I'd like a spell of independence. Hatch my own schemes, and p'r'aps get you to help me carry 'em out. But that's for the future, George—and we seem to have got a long way from that woman's cry—which you now know could not have come all the way across Europe from Black's wife. Of course, it may have been from somebody else's wife.'

'Why don't we go and see?' suggested George, rather obviously.

'We will in a few moments,' answered Smith, 'but do you know, the longer I stay here, the less I feel in a hurry to move. And the reason for that, Georgie, is because I feel pretty convinced that our next move is going to be bang on top of the volcano!'

'All right, but if we're staying don't let's waste time,' retorted George. 'Who is the somebody else's wife? Not yours, by any chance?'

'Not by any chance,' Smith replied, 'though I don't mind admitting that for a very pleasant period she ought to have been. No, I passed her on to our mutual friend Wavell—and Wavell, as you know, *has* got a wife. One who could give him a pretty hot time if she ever came to know of it!'

'So *that's* 'ow they roped 'im in!' thought the corpse on the floor. 'I've 'eard o' that one! Gal let's a bloke love 'er and then sez you do wot I tells yer or I'll blow the gaff ter the missus! Gawd, if this tickle don't stop I'll bust!'

Meanwhile Smith was continuing, 'I can't see what the Chief would want to make Glamorous Gertie squeal for, though. She's doing her stuff too well for any neckwringing.'

George responded, 'P'r'aps the Chief's fallen for the glamour, and what you thought you heard was Gertie objecting!'

Smith laughed. 'That's the worst guess you ever made, George! The Chief could no more fall for glamour than Gertie would object if he did! No, there's another woman we haven't mentioned yet.'

'Who?'

'One who called on our new caretaker here yesterday. I wish I'd got more than a glimpse of her! She was supposed to have come by mistake to the wrong door, but suppose she didn't? And though she didn't get in that time, suppose she's got in since?'

'You didn't recognise her from the glimpse?'

'Not at the time. But I've been thinking, and an impression is growing in my mind that she and I have met before!'

'Where? Same place as Glamorous Gertie?'

'Oh, dear, no! Nothing like that!'

'Then where?'

'I'll keep that under my hat for a moment, George, in case I'm wrong. But if I'm not wrong—if this woman is the young lady I think she is—and if she *has* got in, it wouldn't surprise me in the least if she never got out again . . . Hey, what's happening to our corpse! Hold him!'

24

Ben Bounces

Ben often wondered what would have happened, and whether his twenty-four hours' nightmare would have ended differently if his tickle had not beaten him. 'S'pose, fer instance,' he asked himself, 's'pose I'd kep' me grip on it till it 'ad went away—' for tickles do very occasionally oblige in this surprising manner '—would they of fahnd aht I wasn't dead and finished me orf like, or if they 'adn't fahnd aht would they of rolled me orf somewhere, and if so where, and then wot?' The if's of this hazardous life which seems to take its course from trivial details are as unfathomable as they are uncountable, and so it was not likely that Ben would be able to fathom them.

But the tickle did beat him, and if a world war had resulted, he had to deal with it. A finger of the hand nearest his nose was almost within scratchable distance, but almost is not quite, as he discovered when he had extended it to its extreme limit. Just half-an-inch short! A mere half-inch from heaven; for the joy of ending a tickle even surpasses the agony that preceded the cure. It was cruel.

'But I ain't goin' ter move,' vowed Ben, as his perspiring forehead grew damper and damper against the cold stone floor. 'No, I ain't! See, if I move, it's orl over, and I gotter git Miss Bretherton aht o' this, I jest gotter, well, ain't I, so see, that's settled, I ain't goin' ter move.'

And then, the very next instant, he did move. Body beat spirit, and his extended finger covered the final half-inch to his despairing nose. It did not slide quietly, as it might have attempted under mental direction. There was no mind in the operation, only physical necessity, and it lurched violently like a suddenly released spring.

It was this movement that had brought Smith's attention back to the corpse.

Once Ben had started moving, he did not stop. The finger on the trigger nose had fired the rest of him. Bounding up with the primitive instinct of self-preservation, his tickle forgotten, his physical condition ignored, he dashed away into the darkness before Smith or George could hold him. No good to argue that he couldn't have done it. (Later, he argued that way himself.) He did do it. And wot yer done, yer done. Once again Ben had achieved the impossible.

When a bullet is fired, and that is all Ben was just now—a human bullet—it has no power to direct its course, but goes where it must. If it hits anything soft, it penetrates. If it is too soft itself to penetrate what it hits, it ricochets. That is what Ben did. He hit and bounced, and when he hit again he bounced again. He began to believe that he would go on doing it for ever. Like Sisyphus, doomed for ever in the world of shade to roll his stone endlessly uphill, so Ben, in this other world of darkness, seemed destined to bounce till the end of Time. In his swooning mind (how often had Ben's mind swooned since that first occasion only yesterday on a park seat!) he watched himself doing it. And because he always tried to be philosophic and make the best of things once there was no way out, he told himself at last that he rather liked it. See, yer doesn't 'ave ter do nothink. Yer jest goes on like a billiard ball.

That was the last thing he told himself till, several centuries later, he found to his amazement that he had actually stopped. Well, well! Think o' that, now! I ain't movin'! So the next thing was to find out why he wasn't moving and why he had stopped.

Soon he discovered. Something was around him. He couldn't see what it was because his head was buried against another part of the something. Not a cold stone floor this time. Sort of warm like. Couldn't be a mother, could it? Long ago he'd had one. He managed to move his head back a little way, and as he did so he discovered that the darkness had gone and now there was light. It came from an electric lamp above him.

But Ben was not looking at the lamp. He was looking at the something that held him. It was the monnertrocity.

25

The Owl

Ben was not given time to dwell on this new, unpleasant development. A door opened behind the monnertrocity who, now fully viewed by Ben for the first time, turned out to be a large hairy man with a monkey face and bare, gorilla-like feet, and a small, spectacled man emerged. The man shot a quick glance at Ben and his captor, without any change of expression—Ben was to learn that his expression never changed—and then went back into the room from which he had come, closing the door after him.

At a movement from Ben, the monnertrocity's encircling arms tightened, and Ben knew that escape was impossible. Even had it been possible, where would he have escaped to? Behind him sounded voices. Approaching and familiar.

'Ah! So you've caught our corpse—well done, Monkey-face,' said Smith. The monnertrocity emitted one of his incoherent gurgles while Smith went on, now addressing the corpse, 'You're certainly teaching me things, Jones, and I wish our all-too-short acquaintance were not about to end. For instance, I never knew a dead man could run so fast. I suppose, while you were lying doggo, you heard all we said? Come along! Spill it out! It might be a good idea for you to talk while you still can.'

''Ow can yer tork when yer in a lemon-squeezer?' gulped Ben.

'Let him go, Monkey-face,' ordered Smith, accompanying the order with a gesture. 'He won't do any more running.' The tight embracing arms loosened, and Ben stepped back out of them hastily. 'Whoa! Steady in reverse! You nearly had George over. Now then! To repeat—did you hear all George and I said?'

'I 'eard enuff,' replied Ben.

'That was a pity for you, though I hardly imagine that by this time it will make any difference. You know that is the Chief's door?'

'Oh! And was that 'im wot come aht of it?'

'The Chief never comes out of it. So who did come?'

'Why should I tell yer?'

'Small chap with glasses?'

'Yus, if yer wanter know.'

'That would be the Owl, George. I know the procedure. He came out to see what the din was and now he's inside making his report. He'll be out again shortly—and then what fun!'

As Smith's cynical eyes rested on Ben, he tried to fight back.

''Oo's goin' ter git the fun?' he demanded.

'Well—if the term really applies—you should have a nice little slice of it coming to you.'

'And wot abart *your* slice?'

'Ours? Yes, what about ours, George?'

'We can do without it,' replied George.

'P'r'aps yer'll git it, jest the sime,' retorted Ben. 'Yus, and p'r'aps I won't? It's you wot comes along and mucks things up!'

'Really!' remarked Smith, with raised eyebrows. 'You might explain that?'

'Yer arsked if I 'eard yer torkin'!'

'Yes?'

'Wich I did.'

'So you said. Go on.'

'Leastwise, some of it.'

'Not all?'

'If yer think I was physical fit fer service while I was lyin' at the foot o' them stairs arter me tumble, yer daft!'

'What did you hear, then, that's in your mind at this moment?' asked Smith.

'Well, yer torked abart me a bit, didn't yer?' answered Ben. 'Yus, and I didn't like some o' the things yer said! Lummy, I thort yer'd got me stright by nah, but yer went on as if I was a quitter. S'pose I let on ter the Chief when I sees 'im that *you're* the ones wot's thinkin' o' quittin'?'

Smith's expression darkened, and for the first time Ben thought he had said something to worry him.

'I wouldn't,' advised Smith.

'Why not?'

'Well, for one thing, it mightn't be healthy for you.'

'I see. If I keep mum the Chief'll send me 'ome with a fat cheque and a bottle o' tonic!'

'And for another thing, you'd be talking through your hat and you couldn't prove a word you said.'

'I could charnce that! No 'arm tryin'! If yer still thinks I'm double-crossin', jest pass that on ter the Chief, and see wot *I'll* tell 'im! I'll tell 'im yer goin' ter mike yer pile and then walk aht on 'im—'

A heavy boot came up from the ground and shoved him in the stomach. He fell back, and once more felt the monnertrocity's long arms around him.

'Let's have an accident, Monkey-face,' said Smith. 'Get me? Do that lemon-squeezer act of yours again!'

The long arms tightened. In less than two seconds Ben felt as though all his breath had left him. 'Then yer goes black, doncher?' he thought. He felt himself going black. But before he attained that undesirable hue the arms ceased to squeeze, the door behind the monnertrocity opened again, and the small spectacled man reappeared.

His arrival had a strange psychological effect. As he gazed mildly on the scene, three of those at whom he gazed could have broken his back with ease, and even Ben, refilled with the breath he had lost, could have taken him on; but little though he was, and quiet though his voice when he spoke, the control of the situation had immediately passed to him. Even his lack of expression seemed to give him dominance. Emotion, it implied, was for fools and weaklings.

'What is happening here?' he enquired.

The question was addressed to Smith.

'That's what we're here to find out,' replied Smith.

'I speak of the present moment,' answered the little man, whom Smith had referred to as the Owl. There was something owl-like in his pale eyes. 'I have come to take this man to the Chief.' He indicated Ben with a slight movement of his head. 'Had I come a few moments later, would that still have been possible?'

'We won't argue,' said Smith. 'We want to see the Chief ourselves.'

'I have no doubt he would like to see you. Step inside, if you please.'

He moved from the doorway to allow the little procession to pass through. Smith and George went first, the monnertrocity followed. Ben, the fourth in order, paused as he was about to pass the Owl who was bringing up the rear. He had an uneasy sensation that he had finished with Smith and George, and that unless he was to become quite friendless he must make a bid for the Owl's confidence.

'We ain't the fust visitors terday, are we?' he said, with a not very successful wink. He did not feel in a winking mood.

'Go in,' ordered the Owl.

'I'm goin' in,' answered Ben, and dropped his voice to a whisper. 'It's them others yer wanter watch!'

'We watch everybody,' replied the Owl. 'Even you.'

'That's right,' nodded Ben, affecting approval. 'Yer carn't be too careful in this gime. I expeck there's a cupple *more* 'ere yer watchin', too, ain't there?'

'Your business is with the Chief, not with me. Please do not delay any longer.'

'Okay. I git yer. But if you'd bin through wot I bin through, fallin' dahn stairs and then bein' squeezed like yer was a lemon, yer wouldn't mind a breather yerself!'

Then he went in, and heard the Owl following him and locking the door.

The space they were now in was small, and the five men almost filled it. There was as yet no sign of the Chief, and Ben deduced that this was a sort of ante-room. Like where yer 'ad ter waite at dentists' 'ouses afore yer 'ad yer tooth aht. Now threading his way through the little crowd, the Owl passed through another door, to return almost immediately. He beckoned to Smith and George, made a sign to the monnertrocity, and a moment later Ben found himself alone with Monkey-face.

A tête-à-tête with this unpleasant creature would not have been Ben's choice, but with relief he noticed that the monnertrocity was no longer in a menacing mood. Indeed, the eyes that watched Ben were rather mournful, and if Ben could have been sure that the sadness was not due to frustrated desire, he might have been a little sorry for him. 'Lummy, I ain't nothink ter look at,' he reflected, 'but s'pose I'd bin born like 'im? And then not bein' able ter 'ear or tork, it'd give yer the pip!'

There were no chairs. They stood and waited. Once Ben made a movement towards the entrance door, thinking it would be a good idea to study it for the next time he might want to use it, but a growl from the monnertrocity warned him, and he resumed his static pose. If he once gave his gaoler an excuse to get nasty, there was no knowing just how nasty he would get!

As the minutes dragged by it dawned upon Ben that perhaps he was missing his last opportunity to formulate a plan. Once he found himself in the presence of the mysterious individual referred to as the Chief things would assumedly happen, and while things are happening is not the best time for clear thought. It is only by thinking before things happen that you stand any chance of making them happen the way you want. So while Ben and the monnertrocity stood facing each other, Ben's mind passed beyond his hairy gaoler into the realms of strategy.

'The fust thing,' he decided, 'is ter find aht where Miss Bretherton is. The second thing is ter find aht where Mr Black is. But corse I ain't goin 'ter waist no time on

Mr Black, 'cos arter orl 'oo's 'e any'ow, 'e may be a bad egg 'iself, no, I ain't goin 'ter waist no time on 'im not if I finds Miss Bretherton and spots a charnce o' gittin' 'er aht o' this Gawd-knows-where! Yus, and where *is* it? I reckon this is one o' them air-raid funk-'oles wot was bombed wot's bin turned inter a crooks' 'otel. Where've I got ter? Oh, yus, I'm findin' aht where they are. 'Ow do I do it? By goin' on pertendin'. Wot's goin' ter be the good o' that? I mean, jest pertendin'? That ain't goin' ter git yer nowhere, yer gotter *do* somethink! Think o' somethink, think o' somethink ter do! 'Ow's this? "Yer must be a bit short'anded, Chief, with orl these new people ter look arter," I sez ter 'im. "Monkey-fice carn't look arter the lot." "Yer've sed it," 'e sez. "Then why not mike use o' me," I sez, "and let me keep a eye on the gal?" And then p'r'aps, sayin' we're gittin' on orl right, p'r'aps 'e might give us a wink and say, "If yer was keepin' a eye on the gal there might 'ave ter be some'un ter keep a eye on *you*," meanin' ter be funny, and then I larf, ter flatter 'im like, and we fixes it up. Okay. So then wot? Well, that'd be a start, any'ow, and when yer don't know nothink yer carn't go further than the start. Orl right. That's ter say if 'e believes me. But s'pose 'e don't? 'E mightn't nah, if Smith and George 'ave stopped doin' it—I expeck they're torkin' ter 'im abart me nah, blarst 'em! Well, then, say 'e don't? Wot abart this? I manidges ter git up close ter 'im and pertend ter sneeze—see, the sneeze comin' might sorter tip me t'ords 'im like—and then dahn goes me 'ead, and up it comes wallop in 'is fice . . .'

'Don't you hear me?'

It was the Owl's voice. The door through which the others had passed had reopened, and the ordeal of waiting was over. Ben brought his mind back from the indefinite future to the definite present with a jerk.

'For the third time, come,' said the Owl.

'Oh!' blinked Ben. 'Yer mean me or Tarzan?'

'If you refer to your companion, I mean both,' replied the Owl.

'I see. Yer ready? Well, so'm I. As a matter o' fack, I was jest thinkin' o' the Chief when yer come in and lookin' forward ter seein' 'im.'

'The Chief, I can assure you, is looking forward to seeing you,' replied the Owl.

His expressionless face as he said it reminded Ben less of an owl than an octopus.

26

Conference at Top Level

Out of one door, along a low passage, in through another door—and at long last Ben found himself in the august presence of the Chief.

Unlike in the case of the monnertrocity, who was also present at the queer interview that followed, Ben had not visualised the Chief in his imagination. There is a saturation point beyond which imagination refuses to function, and the large black-haired, bearded, leather-faced man who sat at a big desk—Ben wondered how such a massive piece of furniture had been brought down there—did not therefore upset any preconceived conception. But this did not alter the fact that the Chief's general aspect was supremely disappointing, and it was quite impossible to conceive this grim and sinister figure indulging in a wink!

Oddly, in spite of the disparity in size, the Chief and the Owl made an appropriate pair, for they shared the characteristic of expressionlessness that was predominant in each. From neither inscrutable visage could be deduced what the mind behind was thinking, and even the words spoken by these two Sphinxlike men were not always as informative to Ben as they might have been. The Owl's voice was as expressionless as his face, seeming often to cloak the reason and meaning of what he said, while what the Chief said was completely incomprehensible since he spoke in a foreign tongue. Whether he understood English or not, he never once used it, addressing all his remarks to the Owl for interpretation.

Ben was gestured to a chair a little way from the desk. The Owl sat down in a chair between. The monnertrocity stood behind Ben's chair, patiently awaiting his next instructions. The sole consolation in this over-disciplined atmosphere was that at least it kept the monnertrocity in order.

For a few moments after the four inmates of the Chief's sanctum had settled themselves, no word was spoken. Ben wondered whether this were the usual practice—see, it gits on yer nerves like, which'd be wot they wanted, wouldn't it?—and whether perhaps Miss Bretherton and Mr Black had sat in this very chair before him to endure a similar nerve test? It made you feel you wanted to say something, just to break the silence, but without in the least helping you to know what to say. What Ben said, after the situation had beaten him, was 'Good arternoon,' which somehow did not seem at all right. Indeed, it produced no response from either the Chief or the Owl, so after another period of silent strain Ben tried again.

'When are we goin' ter begin?' he asked.

Then the Owl said, 'We are waiting for you,' and once more relapsed into silence.

This was a new technique to Ben, and he did not know what to do with it.

'Yer mean, yer ain't goin' ter arsk me questions?' he enquired. 'That I gotter start like?'

'That is so,' replied the Owl.

Although, up to now, the Chief had not spoken, Ben felt conscious of the perfect understanding between the two men. The Owl was merely the voice of the Chief.

'I see,' answered Ben, though he didn't. 'Well, wotcher want me ter say?'

'What you have got to say,' came the response.

And then, all at once, instead of being oppressed by the procedure, Ben wondered whether this might not be his big chance? He was being invited to talk. And Smith and George were not present to hear him.

'Okay,' he said. 'Then 'ere goes! I got a complaint!' He paused for somebody to say, 'Have you?' but nobody did. 'See, it's like this. I ain't goin' ter say nothink abart the way I was roped inter orl this, 'cos I expeck yer knows orl abart that as much as I does, and wot Mr Smith did 'e was actin' for yer. We'll let that go. I ain't one ter bear a grudge, and arter orl, wot's 'avin' a little thing like a murder plarnted on yer? We carn't be pertickler in our line, can we? Matter o' fack, I've finished orf 'arf a dozen in my time, so 'oo am I ter tork?'

He paused again for approval, and again received none. The Chief and the Owl exchanged glances, but since the glances lacked expression they did not tell Ben anything, though assumedly they told plenty to each other.

'Orl right,' Ben went on, doggedly. 'That's okay by me. But wot 'appens when I gits 'ere? Ain't yer got no records? Yer'd think blokes like you would 'ave records. You know! Jim Green, cupple o' murders. Billy Brahn, three yards o' pearls and the end o' Policeman X. And then me—but yer don't know! I 'ave ter tell yer! And this is s'posed ter be Number One set-up south o' Scotland!'

Was he overdoing it? He had no idea. If only those two fathomless faces had shown *something*! If an eye had winked or a nose twitched! Well, if they didn't, if his audience remained static, he had to flow on.

'Orl right! Wot 'appens is this! I'm brort 'ere, but I ain't trusted. Me, wot's wanted in more countries than yer 'ave fingers to cahnt 'em! That 'urt! We got our pride, ain't we? 'Ow'd *you* like it if some'un tried ter mike aht yer'd got wings? But I stood it. Do yer know, the one called George pertended ter be a pleeceman ter try and ketch me aht? It's a fack! If I knowd 'oo it was—corse, mindyer, I didn't, 'cos if I 'ad it wouldn't of bin no test, would it, if yer git me?—but if I'd knowd, lummy, I'd 'ave sloshed 'im one! Yus, and when I sloshes, I sloshes!'

He raised a clenched fist and glared at it with what he hoped was ferocity.

'But this mornin' I thort they got over orl that,' he continued. 'Well, they *'ad,* 'cos ain't I give that there packet fer that there Mr Wavell when 'e calls at 10.30 with that there Mr Black, and would they of done that if I wasn't ter be trusted? Orl right. And so—well, wot 'appens ter Mr Black was wot yer wanted ter 'appen ter 'im, yus, and—' He paused, gulped, and went on, 'Yus, and aincher got that lidy, too—aincher?—that's a fack, ain't it? And orl 'cos the way I bin helpin' yer! And *then* wot? Yus, and nah I'm comin' ter it, Chief!' He had been looking at the Owl, finding that easier than looking at the Chief, but now he jerked his head round and faced the Chief bravely. 'I expect Smith and George 'ave been spinnin' the yarn ter yer, 'cos yer 'ad 'em in fust, but nah 'ere's *my* yarn, and

I'm tellin' yer! If they didn't trust me, I didn't trust *them*!
Not when I sees 'ow things is goin'. And so when I 'as a
accident fallin' dahn some stairs, and 'ears' em torkin' ter
theirselves when I comes to, I pertends ter be dead, and I
'ears 'em saying they're goin' ter cut loose once they've
mide their little pile aht o' you. They don't like yer methods,
they sez. I couldn't tell yer orl they sed, me marth would
go on strike! Yus, and when they learns I ain't dead, but
am goin' ter spill the beans ter you, wot 'appens?'

He swung round. 'Arsk Monkey-fice! Yus, and arsk the
Owl! . . . Eh? . . .' Lummy, that was a slip, wasn't it?
'That's wot they calls yer, sir,' he gulped, now turning to
the Owl. 'The Owl! 'Ow's that fer cheek? Any'ow, *you*
saw, didn't yer, 'ow they give me ter Monkey-fice ter finish
me orf, so's I couldn't split on 'em! The Chief 'ad sent fer
me, but they wanted ter finish me orf fust—and they would
of if you 'adn't come along, jest like yer sed! . . . Well, is
that enuff? Or do yer want any more?'

Now for the first time, the Chief spoke. As all Ben knew
outside his own language was Orrivore, what the Chief
said was unintelligible to him, and so, for a little while,
was what the Owl said. They had a short conference, in
low toneless voices, and then the Chief sat back in his chair
and folded his arms, while the Owl turned back to Ben.

'We have heard what you have told us,' said the Owl,
impassively. 'Is there anything more?'

'If I've left anythink aht,' returned Ben, 'you tell me!'

'You mentioned a packet.'

'The one I was ter give ter Mr Wavell?'

'You mentioned it, but not what was in it.'

'I wasn't s'posed ter know. There yer are! Not trusted
agine!'

207

'Did you know?'

'I'd of 'ad ter open it.'

'Did you open it?'

'Corse not. Wot would I of fahnd if I 'ad?'

The Chief said something. The Owl translated.

'A needle.'

'Oh,' said Ben. 'It was a big packet for a needle. Did Mr Wavell 'ave a button orf?'

'It was not that sort of needle.'

'Wot sort was it then?'

'You should know.'

'Why?' But as Ben asked the question, he realised the answer. 'It was the sime as wot I 'ad put in me yesterday in the park.'

'It was.'

'I see. And Mr Wavell put it inter Mr Black.'

'He did.'

''Cos Mr Black wouldn't do wot 'e was told?'

'What is your opinion about that?'

'Well, that's wot it looks like, don't it?'

'We agree it might have that appearance.'

'Wot was it,' asked Ben, 'that Mr Black wouldn't do?'

The Owl waited till the Chief spoke. Then, again, he translated.

'He needed an inducement to complete the business he had come for.'

'I ain't good at long words, but I git yer,' said Ben. 'Is the business done nah?'

'It interests you?'

'Well, ain't I in it?'

Another pause. Another remark by the Chief. Another translation.

'You are in it. Up to the neck. The business is not quite completed.'

Ben hoped that no one but himself knew of the cold chill that went through him.

'It's—goin' ter be—eh?'

'Undoubtedly, it is going to be.'

'Yer've—yer've got 'im sife like?'

'Mr Black will not leave here until the business is finished.'

'And wot abart—the other one?'

'Meaning?'

'The lidy.'

'We have her safely here, too.'

'Along o' Mr Black?'

'Along with Mr Black.'

'Yer mean, they're tergether like?'

The Owl glanced towards the Chief. The Chief nodded. After so much immobility, the nod seemed almost like a violent motion.

'They are together.'

The Chief made another remark.

'The arrival of the lady,' translated the Owl, 'will assist the completion of the business.'

What did that mean? It had a wretchedly sinister sound. Trying to conceal his anxiety, Ben asked,

'Did yer 'ave ter use the needle on 'er?'

'No, we did not,' replied the Owl.

''Ow was that?'

'Women are notoriously curious.'

'I don't git yer?'

'The cellar door was open.'

'Oh! Some'un fergot ter lock it?'

'No.'

Light dawned.

'Yer mean, it wasn't locked on purpose?'

'That is the meaning.'

'And she jest walked in.'

'As you did yourself.'

'Nah I git yer. Keep orf when yer ain't wanted, but come along when yer are.'

'Quite nicely put.'

'Well, I ain't Shakespeare,' said Ben, modestly, 'but I gits there with words sometimes. One o' the doors that was open, wot I calls the cubbard door, that 'un closed arter I gorn through it.'

'That was closed,' replied the Owl, 'from here.'

'Go on!'

'I hope you now think a little more of our organisation?'

'Eh?'

'In spite of the fact that we did not have your name on our list?'

'Ferget it,' said Ben, generously. 'You know a bit!' He felt he was getting along rather well, and a little more buttering-up might do the trick. 'But 'ow did yer know I come through, ter close it be'ind me? That was smart, yer carn't git away from it, 'cos I didn't see nobody there!'

'Nobody was there.'

'Go on!'

The Owl looked towards the Chief, who unfolded his arms and lowered a hand behind the desk. A metallic buzzing sound filled the room for a moment.

'That,' said the Owl, 'is the sound we hear every time anyone passes through that door.'

'I'm blowed!' muttered Ben, and the admiration in his

voice was not entirely feigned. 'It mikes one prahd ter work with yer! Yer 'eard that buzzer agine, arter it sahnded fer me, didn't yer? See, Mr Smith and George was be'ind me.'

'That is so.'

''Ow did they git in, arter the door was closed?'

'It was closed, but not bolted. We expected Smith, but not quite so soon. In spite of our organisation, which you so kindly praise, things have not gone today with their usual smoothness.'

'Well, I'm 'ere ter 'elp yer,' replied Ben, 'and p'r'aps terday'll end better than it begun.'

'And how,' asked the Owl, 'do you propose to help us?'

'Well, corse, that's up ter you,' answered Ben, 'but I got an idea.'

'May we learn it?'

'Yer sed this Mr Black and the lidy was tergether?'

'That is correct.'

'Meanin' they're in the sime room like.'

'That is again correct.'

'Well, yer've 'eard wot I'd told yer abart Mr Smith and George, and yer seen wot yer seen ter corryob it.'

'Corryob?'

'Eh? That means ter mike proof like.'

'Corroborate?'

'I ain't 'eard that one, but I expeck it means the sime. Any'ow, yer know they ain't ter be trusted.'

'We know that is your opinion.'

'Well, ain't it your'n?'

'It must occur to you that they have expressed the same opinion about yourself.'

'They would.'

'They have.'

'Lummy! There're times when I carn't mike yer aht,' complained Ben. 'Yer top o' the blinkin' tree, but yer don't know a crook when yer sees one!'

'We are still waiting,' the Owl reminded him, 'to learn how you propose to help us?'

'Oh, yus. Well, this is the way. 'Oo's guardin' Mr Black and Miss—and the lidy?'

'Miss?'

'Eh?'

'You said "miss"?'

'That's right,' agreed Ben, cursing himself for another slip, though he had no idea by now whether this one mattered or not. 'And then I 'ad ter stop 'cos I couldn't go on, not knowin', she might be Mrs Any'ow, 'oo's guardin' 'em?'

'Continue.'

'Well, see, I thort p'r'aps I might keep a eye on 'em—if yer was short'anded?'

This was the plan he had worked out while waiting in the ante-room, though in the original scheme Miss Bretherton had been alone, which would have been preferable, and the Chief had winked at him. But the Chief did not wink at him, and while Ben held his breath there was another interchange between the Chief and the Owl. When it was over, the Owl resumed the conversation along instructed lines.

'It is certainly necessary,' said the Owl, 'that our two visitors do not leave until we decide that they shall do so. If, indeed, we do decide that they shall do so. And, also, if they are in a condition to do so.'

He paused, and Ben's heart stopped beating for a second. He managed to keep his face, however, and even to induce

212

an expression of frozen pleasure to distort it. The effort did not go unnoticed.

'My words please you?'

'That's right,' muttered Ben, thickly. 'We carn't let 'em go.'

'We do not mean to let them go.'

'That's right.'

'Nor even separate, for the beauty of having them both together is that, if the one who has not yet completed his business still refuses to complete it, he will have to watch the other pay the price of his obstinacy.'

Ben moistened his dry lips.

'You follow?' enquired the Owl.

'I git yer,' murmured Ben.

'And still with satisfaction?'

'Corse!'

'And, if we gave you the job of guarding our two visitors, you would guard them safely for the purpose we have in view?'

'Eh?'

'And would gladly be present, with ourselves and our friend just behind you, to continue your assistance while the—business was being concluded?'

The Owl stopped speaking, waiting for Ben's response. Even now, his expression did not change. His eyebrows might at least have been raised, but they remained, with the rest of his features, as if stuck.

Ben just managed to get out the words,

'Why not?'

The Chief said something and passed the Owl a sheet. The Owl took it quietly and read it; then continued.

'We will tell you why not. You have referred to our list.

213

We keep one. And contrary to your expressed belief, you *are* down on it—*now*. Though not precisely in the terms you yourself indicated. Let me mention your record, as we have it here.'

He lowered his eyes to the sheet for a moment.

'I will not give you all the items, for there are far too many for the limited time we have at our disposal, and incidentally they make rather nauseous reading. Three will suffice. In the first, you appear to have become associated with a detective named Gilbert Fordyce at a house numbered, not Nineteen as ours is here, but Seventeen. I have no doubt you recall it. You were instrumental in breaking up an organisation that made use of a railway tunnel.'

'Owjer know that was me?' demanded Ben.

Ignoring the question, the Owl went on.

'In the second, you became too curious in the happenings behind a window opposite your own. In the third— passing over many other occasions and coming now to a much more recent date—you discovered a dead man in the cellar of No. 15, Norgate Road, and instead of leaving well alone, you interfered once more, with disastrous results to members of the fraternity to which you claim to belong. Is it likely that, knowing your record, we should consider you a proper person to guard Mr Black and Miss Bretherton?'

The game seemed up, but Ben held on. This implied neither special grit nor courage. You hold on to a plank while you are sinking.

'Corse, I know 'ow yer've got this orl wrong,' he said. 'Smith and George knew I'd tell on 'em, so they 'as ter try and dish me fust! Me that feller? Wot a larf!'

214

'You know him, then?'

'Know 'im? I met 'im once, and give 'im wot for!'

'The meeting must have been interesting.'

'Yus, and nex' time I meet Smith and George, I'll give *them* wot for!'

'I am afraid you will not have the chance,' remarked the Owl, 'and in any case it was not they who identified you.'

'Oh! Then 'oo did?'

'A lady who met you in one of your many previous episodes, and who has no cause to love you. She saw the photograph that was taken of you yesterday on the park seat—before your transformation—and as she is working for us at the moment she very rightly considered it her duty to tell us what she knew about you.' Ben guessed this to be the siren who had woven her entangling net around Mr Wavell, and for whom Mrs Wavell had mistaken Miss Bretherton in the cupboard. But he was not given time to dwell on such points, for the Owl was continuing in his monotonous, expressionless drone, 'And so, you see, we cannot have *you* working for us any longer, and must terminate our own brief association. One way would be to hand you over to the police for the murder of Bretherton. Oh, yes, we could do this, I have no doubt, with very little risk. But why run any risk at all? The interview is ended. Take him away.'

He made a sign to the monnertrocity, and Ben suddenly found himself lifted from the ground in long, hairy arms.

27

Topsy-Turvy

If you fall in front of a train, and you have time to think about it, you will give yourself up for lost. Then, should you have fallen between the tracks to discover that the train has passed over you with injury only to your nervous system, you will assume that you have been saved by a miracle. This does not mean that the next time you fall in front of a train you will not be equally terrified. Miracles, you will argue, if you have time to argue, do not happen twice.

But suppose you fall in front of a train twenty times? You may still disbelieve in a succession of miracles, but you will at last assume that Fate is looking after you and that you no longer have any cause to worry. And the time you do that will probably be the time Fate throws you on the dust-heap and goes off to look after somebody else.

It was when the monnertrocity took Ben up in its arms— the creature had a gender, but Ben could only think of it as an 'it'—that he came to the conclusion that Fate was looking after him. 'See,' he argued, as with closed eyes he felt himself being borne along Gawd knew where, 'I must of bin nearly dead abart five 'undred times, not cahntin' the nummer o' times in the larst twenty-four hours. Orl right. If I wasn't popped orf any o' them times, why should I be popped orf this 'un? It ain't reasonable! Faite's lookin' arter me, yer carn't git away from it, so 'oo's worryin'?'

Therefore, although it would not be strictly true to say that Ben's mind was happy when at last he felt himself put down and opened his eyes to find that he had been put down on a chair by which the monnertrocity was standing guard, at least he was not in a panic, and was sufficiently composed to take swift note of his new surroundings. The chair, a table, a candle on the table, the monnertrocity, himself, four walls and a closed door, completed the inventory. What did they all add up to?

As they did not add up to anything, it seemed, of which Ben could make any use, he waited for divine inspiration, while the monnertrocity continued to stand and watch him with sadistic anticipating eyes.

Whether what happened next was due to divine inspiration or to the uniqueness of Ben's own mind may be a moot point. We ourselves may be inclined to give Ben full credit, but Ben was as certain that his actions were divinely inspired as he was that they were, even in his incredible experience, unbelievable. Indeed the events which followed were so unbelievable that he was convinced neither his nor any other mortal mind could have thought of them, let alone put them into action.

They were started off by a sudden movement from the monnertrocity. This movement was certainly not divinely inspired, since it bore too strong a resemblance to an animal about to spring on its prey, and it was the movement which this induced in Ben that provided the *pièce de résistance*. He leapt up from his chair, kicked it aside, and stood on his head.

He did not know why he did it until he was in the process of doing it. The discovery came as his head went down and his legs went up. 'I'm doin' this,' he thought, 'ter tike 'is mind orf like!'

It undoubtedly took the monnertrocity's mind off. It also presented him with an anatomical difficulty. It is less easy to throttle a man who is upside down than another who is the right way up, for people do not breathe through their boots.

What, wondered upside-down Ben, would the monnertrocity do now? Once it had overcome its surprise, would it deliver the postponed attack? The next few moments were unbearable, though they had to be borne, the unbearableness being augmented by the fact that, in his inverted position, Ben's direction was also reversed, and he now had his back to the monnertrocity with no capacity to turn his head and look. He only had his ears to judge by, and when after a few seconds he heard a slow shuffling sound, he judged that the creature was moving. The sound drew closer, its one virtue being its slowness.

At first it came towards him. Then it paused. Then it ceased its direct approach, and gradually circled round, till at last the monnertrocity came into view, to pause once more at the extraordinary sight now observed to best advantage.

With less advantage, Ben observed the observer, painfully realising that this strange attempt to solve his immediate problem was a case of kill or cure. Whatever chance he had had of warding off the monnertrocity's attack right side up, he now had no chance at all of warding it off upside down. 'I s'pose wot'll 'appen,' he thought. 'I'll jest go flop, and that'll be that like.'

So he waited to go flop, but he did not go flop. The monnertrocity continued to gaze at the unusual spectacle, and gradually its expression changed from sheer surprise to a new form of interest at first unfathomable. Was it now studying its victim to work out how best to deal with it from this new angle? That was the obvious deduction till it dawned upon Ben that the monnertrocity's expression did not fit into the interpretation, for the expression was no longer menacing. It was intrigued. It said, 'I have never seen such a thing before!' And the monnertrocity never had.

The situation became static. Neither the beholder nor the beheld did anything until at last Ben realised that this could not go on for ever. Not, at any rate, as far as he was concerned. Carefully he brought his legs down to earth again, less through policy than through necessity, and as he did so the monnertrocity's expression changed. At first Ben was unaware of the change, since the operation of descent had brought him with his back to the creature once more. It was not until he had regained his erect position and turned that he saw the monnertrocity's eyes alive with angry disappointment. It emitted a gurgling growl, its only form of speech.

'Wot, didn't yer like it?' asked Ben, apprehensively.

The monnertrocity growled again.

'*You* 'ave a shot?' suggested Ben.

The monnertrocity gestured imperiously towards the floor.

'Lummy! 'E wants me ter do it fer 'im agine!' thought Ben.

Well, better appease him!

So Ben went down for a second performance, and the second performance was as greatly admired as the first. It was, however, a shorter performance, for the performer's head was getting sore, and when it was over Ben looked at the monnertrocity anxiously, hoping he would not demand yet another effort. To his relief there was no immediate indication of this. He found the monnertrocity grinning. This, surely, was a triumph, and, quickly and hard, Ben grinned back to preserve this better humour.

'If we goes on like this,' he thought, ''oo knows we won't end up by kissin'!' As the grinning persisted he became so encouraged that, when the monnertrocity pointed once more to the floor, he shook his head, risked touching the creature on the shoulder, and then pointed to the floor himself.

The unbelievable scene went on. Something had been awakened in the creature's breast, stirring emotions that had never been stirred before. If it had previously lusted for pain, now it lusted for play. Tragedy turned grotesquely into comedy, though there was no knowing how long the comedy would last. Ben had been surprised when he had stood on his head. When, after two or three minutes of inducement and persuasion, the monnertrocity followed suit, he was staggered.

'This ain't true,' he said solemnly, as he watched the great feet rising and waving.

But it was true, and with the undeniable evidence before him he suddenly realised the possibility of turning his negative advantage into a positive one. He had prevented or postponed the monnertrocity's attack. Could he use this moment to become the attacker himself? Yus, 'ow abart goin' fer 'im nah I've got 'im upside dahn?

Two thoughts deterred him. One was that this would mean a return to the war he was trying to avert, and even with this initial advantage Ben doubted whether he would win out in the end. The second thought was, well, would it be cricket? If you're not supposed to hit a man when he's down, you certainly shouldn't hit him when he's upside down! Thus argued Ben, and while he argued the monnertrocity concluded his performance and the chance was lost.

But it very soon became clear to Ben that he had acted wisely in restraining his bellicose impulse, for now the monnertrocity seemed more amiable than ever. In addition to amiability he exuded a childish excitement. The strange noises he emitted and the elevation of his thick eyebrows to their loftiest height so clearly meant, 'Did I do it right?— Was it good?—Am I not clever?' that Ben responded with violent nods of his head, and even pattings on his queer companion's back. The pattings had almost as great effect on the monnertrocity as the performance, for all at once he paused in his antics, as though something had suddenly hit him, and his features took on a new puzzled expression. He blinked first at the hand that had patted him and then at the man who had directed the hand, as though engaged in working out a novel problem. The hand that had patted him could not have done so unless its owner had desired it. Why, then, had the owner desired it? Why, indeed going a little farther back, had the owner shown him this wonderful trick, introducing such entrancing new experience, such stimulating new sensation?

Watching him, and trying to interpret what was happening, Ben thought, 'Ain't nobody never give 'im a friendly pat afore? P'r'aps 'e ain't never 'ad no friend like—yer carn't 'elp feelin' a bit sorry fer 'im!'

Ben's interpretation was sufficiently accurate, for the monnertrocity's world comprised only two sorts of people—those he was afraid of, and those who were afraid of him. It had to be one or the other.

Well, whatever this new sort of person, it was good, and as the monnertrocity's crude mind returned pain for pain, it now urged him to return pleasure for pleasure. Ben steeled himself for the pat he saw coming, and just managed to survive it. It was indeed a volcanic thump, and when Ben had recovered from the shock he was just in time to see the monnertrocity speeding from the room.

'Where's 'e gorn?' he wondered. 'Ter spread the good news?'

Wherever he had gone it seemed a good idea to follow, for with luck the monnertrocity might lead Ben to where he desired to go, while at worst it would be useful to know where the fellow had parked himself. A further indication of the monnertrocity's new mood lay in the fact that the door was wide and it had no longer seemed necessary to lock the prisoner in. As Ben reached the passage the unmistakable sound of the monnertrocity's feet gave him the direction.

He followed cautiously. Even though things were going so surprisingly well he meant to take no chances. He'd seen boxers get the k.o. through over-confidence, and the only time he'd ever had over-confidence himself he'd walked smack into oblivion. The sound of the steps took him round a dark corner—wot a maze this was, yer couldn't git away from it!—and then round another. Then, for a nasty moment, he lost himself. But all at once, as he rounded yet another corner, he heard voices, while between him and the voices loped the monnertrocity.

At first the voices were too faint to decipher, but soon the words became clearer, and just before the monnertrocity reached the doorway through which the voices were sounding, Ben recognised the expressionless tone of the Owl.

'You can put him out of your mind, Miss Bretherton,' the Owl was saying, 'for by this time there is no need for him to remain in ours.'

Miss Bretherton's response came sharply. 'What do you mean?'

The Owl replied, 'I mean that he has been dealt with. He has been dealt with in the same way that you yourself will be dealt with, when our man returns, if the Professor continues to persist in his reticence . . . One moment.'

The Chief's voice interposed here, and when he had finished the Owl translated, speaking as unemotionally as though he were mentioning some small domestic detail.

'I am corrected. It will not be in quite the same manner, though the end will be the same. The process will be slower. You have already had one small sample. You did not appear to like it very much. You will like the rest less. Ah, and here comes our man, just when he is wanted.'

As these words were spoken, the monnertrocity slipped out of Ben's view through the doorway.

'And now, Professor, the next move is with you . . . Yes, yes, wait a moment, wait a moment.' Was there, for the first time, a slight change in the Owl's monotone? The words, at least, had an impatient savour, and Ben wondered, with perspiring forehead and fists clenched, whether they were addressed to the monnertrocity, and if so what had evoked them? Ben knew that communication between the monnertrocity and his employers had been brought to

223

a fine art, and that the words would have been accompanied by the appropriate signs and gestures. 'Well, Professor, what is it to be?'

'Are you devils?'

That was Mr Black's voice. Mr Black, then, was the Professor.

'We merely ask you to complete the business which brought you here,' answered the Owl. 'We did anticipate the possibility of trouble—that when you got here you might weaken and change your mind. As indeed you did. Others have done it before you. That was why we had, so to speak, to assist you in. But now I am to tell you that we are no longer in a mood to waste time. I will put it more clearly. We are not in a position to. We must have your information to pass on at once, for the Chief has been summoned by an even Higher Authority—and our present address is about to change . . . What is the matter with you? Cannot you stay still for a moment? . . . Excuse this interruption, Professor, but you will note that our man seems to be growing impatient, so from every angle you must decide on your course immediately. The alternatives are plain. You will give us your information, or Miss Bretherton here—and your wife elsewhere—will have to suffer for your broken word. There is no need to mince matters. The choice is yours, and I speak plainly to assist your decision. Well?'

One can only die once, saving in imagination, and Ben prepared to die now as he slid right up to the door which the monnertrocity had not troubled to close. But he meant to do all the damage he could before being damaged himself beyond repair, and his fists were so tightly clenched that his knuckles showed white. The sight he glimpsed through the doorway, however, caused him to pause.

All eyes, including Ben's, were on the monnertrocity. Just as Ben had diverted this creature by standing on his head, so now did the creature divert by the same means six others from their grim business—the Chief, the Owl, Smith and George, who had been silent spectators of the preceding scene, the Professor, and Miss Bretherton. They were all staring in complete astonishment at the unexpected sight, and were so intent on it that Ben, now standing in full view in the doorway, was unnoticed.

'What—the devil—!' came a mutter from Smith.

'I fear,' said the Owl, 'our friend has now gone finally out of his mind.'

'Look out!' cried George.

For the monnertrocity had abruptly retrieved his normal position and leapt towards Smith, pointing to the ground as he did so. Smith backed away. Disappointed, the monnertrocity turned to George with the same result. George also backed, refusing to oblige. Anger now began to mingle with the creature's disappointment, and as he moved forward and made a grab, George ducked and struck.

Ben seized the moment. As a rule he did all the wrong things, but now he seemed to be doing all the right ones, and he realised that if he could take advantage of the monnertrocity's irate mood he might turn a former foe into an active ally. With a roar he hurled himself at the astonished George. The monnertrocity, recognising his former playmate and contrasting him favourably with the rest of the company, joined in this new game and hurled himself at Smith, but in a few moments the lust for fun was swamped by the lust for battle, and pandemonium reigned.

Somehow Ben kept his head. 'Git 'er aht quick!' he shouted as the Professor was about to join in the fray. The

Professor kept his head, too, and seizing Miss Bretherton's arm made for the door as a shot rang out. It came from the Chief. 'Gawd, 'urry!' yelled Ben. 'I'm arter yer!' He said it to get rid of them, as he saw Miss Bretherton waver, but he did not believe it, for the Chief's revolver was now directed towards him. 'I 'ope 'e 'it's me in the middle,' thought Ben, ''cos then it'll be quick!' He just had time to land a beauty on Smith's chin—that would make a nice last memory—when the bullet came. But it did not hit Ben in the middle. It hit the swooping monnertrocity. Ben heard him drop with a thud.

Ben wanted to stop, but his legs wouldn't let him. 'I fergive yer fer the cat!' he wept, and fled out through the darkness.

A third shot followed him.

28

The Nightmare Chimes Out

Ben laughed. When somebody asked him why, he did not trouble to find out who it was, but went on laughing. At least, he supposed the laughter was coming from him, but of course it might be someone else. You never knew. You never knew anything.

Presently he explained.

'Mind yer, it ain't really funny,' he said, 'but a thing don't orlways 'ave ter be funny ter git yer. 'Ave yer ever seed a chicken runnin' abart withaht it's 'ead? Well, that ain't funny, but it gits yer.'

'How about going to sleep again, and telling us another time?' came the suggestion.

That was another somebody, but Ben still didn't trouble about identities. Plenty of time for that when the mists cleared.

'Go ter sleep agine? No thanks!' he answered whoever-it-was. 'That's wot I was larfin' abart! When yer goes ter sleep yer never knows where yer goin' ter wike up, and I've 'ad enuff o' that fer a month o' Sundays! Fust it's a bed, and then it's a kitching floor, and then it's a staircaise, and then it's the bottom of another staircaise, and nah it's a cooch! Lummy, if I goes ter sleep agine, nex' time it'll be atop of a 'ay-stack!'

Then, suddenly, the mists cleared. That was how it generally happened with Ben. Fust, everythink's fur-orf like, and then *bing*! it gits close so quick it almost 'its yer! He found himself staring at Miss Bretherton and the Professor.

'Oh! It's you,' he blinked.

'How are you feeling?' asked Miss Bretherton.

'I orlways thort Perfessers 'ad beards,' said Ben. As the Professor and Miss Bretherton exchanged glances he added, 'It's orl right, I often gits funny thorts, it don't matter. Wot 'appened?'

'Are you quite sure you're ready to talk?'

'Well, yer goin' ter do the torkin', aincher?'

'True. But drink this first.'

Ben took the glass that was handed to him, and downed the contents obediently. The contents were a bit disappointing, but they did their job.

'I'll begin, shall I?' said Miss Bretherton, addressing her question to the Professor, who nodded. She turned back to Ben. 'After all, I've not very much to tell, and you may know or guess most of it. Do you know what happened to me when you went upstairs to see if the coast was clear? After we'd decided to try for the police?'

'I knows yer was gorn when I come dahn agine,' replied Ben, 'and as the back door was bolted I knew yer 'adn't gorn aht. Did the—the monnertrocity pop aht of the cellar and git yer?'

She smiled faintly at the Professor's enquiring look.

'That is what he calls the hairy deaf-mute,' she told him.

'Ah, Tarzan,' murmured the Professor.

'Yes, it was Tarzan who jumped out at me, Ben, only a few moments after you'd gone upstairs. He was so quick there wasn't even time to scream—and he had his large hand over my mouth, anyway. He carried me through the cellar to the man they called the Chief and his interpreter, but I don't remember much for a bit—not until they brought you in, Professor.' She shuddered. 'It was a horrible moment!'

'For me, too,' returned the Professor. 'I guessed their devilish design. And when that hideous creature began to—'

'Please don't talk about it!' she interrupted. 'Luckily— thanks to Ben—I was only given that one sample! You see,' she turned to Ben again, 'that first interview in the Chief's room was interrupted. I'm not quite clear about all that happened, but we were sent away when the other two men arrived, and not brought back until just before you and—your Monnertrocity turned up. Well—isn't that all? You know the rest—but did you understand it?' She shook her head. 'Whatever made him act as he did? Though thank God for it!'

'Yus, I can tell yer that,' answered Ben.

'Can you?'

'See, I showed 'im 'ow.' They stared at him while he explained. 'It was arter the Chief 'ad finished with me, arter I'd gorn in through the cellar arter you—'

'How did *you* get in?' interrupted Miss Bretherton.

'Eh? Oh, well, see, I fahnd orl the doors unlocked. I expeck they was too bizzy with you and Mr Black—least-wise that's wot 'e called 'iself fust, ain't it, so that's wot I called 'im—any'ow I expeck they was too bizzy with you ter send the monnertrocity arter me that time, and corse them other two 'adn't turned up yet, bein' be'ind me, so they lef' the doors unlocked knowin' I'd come arter yer sime as a mouse goes arter cheese, yer don't 'ave ter fetch 'em to it, do yer? So in I goes, and dahn I tumbles, and when I come to I'm took orf ter the Chief and the Owl—'

'Owl?'

'Eh? That's the one yer calls the intrumpeter, any'ow that's where I was took arter the tumble and 'earin' yer scream, lummy, that 'urt me 'most as much as it 'urt you, well, in a manner o' speakin', and jest when I thinks I'm gittin' 'em ter berlieve I'm a wrong 'un, so's I can git 'em ter tike me ter you, I finds they're on'y pullin' me leg, like they jest wanted nothink more'n ter 'ear me tork—'

'They would hardly wish to miss that,' murmured the Professor, softly.

'Eh?'

'Nothing. Please go on.'

'Well, there ain't much more,' continued Ben, 'leastwise not till we comes up ter the part wot yer knows where I joined yer. See, the monnertrocity 'ad took me away some-wheres ter finish me orf, that's wot 'appened ter everybody wot knew too much—yer remember, miss, I warned yer abart that, didn't I?—and then, orl of a suddin, jest as 'e was gittin' ready ter spring on me and I was sayin' good-bye ter life like and thinkin' 'as it bin fun or 'as it?—well, then I gits wot's called a hinserpaishun, and if Gawd didn't put it inside o' me, arsk me another! Do yer remember me torkin' abart wot's called maikin' a divvishun? It was when we was tryin' ter think o' ways o' gittin' ter the pleece?'

Miss Bretherton nodded. For the moment she was

speechless before Ben's onrush of words, and with the Professor was trying to keep up with them.

'Well, that's wot I did, miss. I mide a divvishun. I stood on me' ead, and yer orter've seed the monnertrocity's fice! Corse, I couldn't see it meself not afore 'e come rahnd fer a closer look, see, when yer stands on yer 'ead yer finds yerself lookin' t'other way, and if yer don't git me, try it, but any'ow it did the trick, and ter keep it orl goin' like I got 'im ter stand on 'is 'ead, and 'e was so pleased 'e almost kissed me!' He paused for an instant, and his voice was a little shaky as he went on. 'Yer know—it's funny—but yer gotter know a bloke ter find aht orl abart 'im, aincher—and then, arter 'e gits ter know you, too—corse, yer both gotter do it—' He paused again, and swallowed. 'Well, any'ow, 'stead o' goin' fer me, orf 'e trots ter do 'is new trick ter the rest of yer, and corse I follers. 'E wanted ter see the 'ole lot 'ave a go, 'e'd 'ave bin on ter you nex'. But—well, yer knows wot 'appened arter that. On'y p'r'aps there's one thing yer don't know.'

'What was that?' asked the Professor, quietly.

'If it 'adn't bin fer the monnertrocity,' replied Ben, 'I wouldn't be 'ere. Wherever 'ere is.'

'My flat,' Miss Bretherton told him. 'You mean if he hadn't changed his mind about killing you?'

'No, miss. I mean if 'e 'adn't jumped atween me and the Chief when the Chief 'ad a pot at me arter missin' *you*. Corse,' said Ben, reflectively, 'it might of jest 'appened that way, yer never know, but on the other 'and 'e might of meant ter do it fer me. You know, us nah bein' friends like. Well, come ter that, p'r'aps I'd of done the sime fer 'im—in spite o' wot 'e done ter the cat. Yer never know, do yer? Not in a crissis. If yer git me?'

'I get you, Ben,' said Miss Bretherton.

Suddenly Ben exclaimed, 'Yus, but 'arf a mo'! The Chief 'ad another pot at me jest as I was comin' aht arter you—and *that* one 'it me! So why ain't I dead?'

Now the Professor took up the story.

'It did not hit you,' he said.

'Go on! I never walked 'ere!'

'No. You were carried—at least, the first part of the journey. That third bullet grazed you but it did not hit you, and you may have collapsed through the shock of thinking you were dead. Not very surprising after all you had been through.'

Ben nodded. 'That's right, sir. It's become a 'abit. I didn't need no doctor, then, eh?'

'My own medical knowledge is sufficient. I began my career as a doctor. Then—well, I became more interested in science. I wonder, now, if that suggests anything to you?'

Ben found the Professor's eyes fixed on him with grim enquiry.

'Do yer mean, sir,' he answered, as certain recent newspaper headlines passed through his mind, 'that yer was goin' ter be one o' them Disappearin' Perfessers like?'

'But for you,' came the dry response, 'I should certainly have disappeared, although not perhaps in the form originally intended. What would you say if I told you that much of the Chief's business was connected with disappearing professors—and others as well, for that matter—and that when you opened the door to me this morning I was expected to pass some very valuable scientific information on to a foreign power?'

Ben fished in his mind uncomfortably for the right reply.

'What would you say?' repeated the Professor. 'You appear to have some ethical code.'

'I dunno wot that is,' answered Ben, 'but p'r'aps I'd say I was lucky not ter 'ave a wife, 'cos, see, I on'y got meself ter worry abart.'

The Professor turned to Miss Bretherton with a smile. 'He whitewashes everybody,' he remarked.

'There's a packet in Nummer Nineteen I wouldn't whitewash with a barge pole!' he denied. 'Wot's 'appened to 'em?'

'They are no longer in No. 19. I don't know what has happened to the Chief and his interpreter, but the other two are in the hands of the police.'

'Go on!'

'That should not surprise you. I expect they knew the game was up, and in their effort to escape they kindly opened doors for us.'

'Well, well! Wotcher know abart that?' He asked, hopefully, 'Does that mean, sir, we can nah drop aht of it?'

'Well, not quite at once,' replied the Professor. 'We've got to make our statements and give our evidence, you know, and to have them accepted. I'd better tell you that a police sergeant is waiting below at this moment, to come up when you are ready for him.'

'Oh, is 'e? 'Ow nice!' muttered Ben. 'And s'pose my heavidunce ain't accepted?' His mind harped back to the start of it all, and he turned to Miss Bretherton. 'Yer ain't fergot them finger-prints o' mine, miss, wot Smith planted on the knife wot killed yer brother?'

'Don't worry about that, Ben,' she answered. 'There's too much else in your favour. Do you feel ready for that policeman now? To get it over?' She added with a smile, 'I've taken off your side-whiskers.'

Ben grinned back. 'I wunnered why my cheeks was cold!'

The Professor left the room. As he did so, a clock on the mantelpiece chimed the hour. Ben switched his body round to stare at the clock-face unbelievingly.

'What's the matter?' asked Miss Bretherton.

'Lummy—that was four o'clock—the time it begun!' he blinked. ''As it orl 'appened in twenty-four hours? . . . Go on!'

THE END